IN THE HANDS OF ANUBIS

IN THE
HANDS
OF ANUBIS

ANN ERIKSSON

LIBRARY AND ARCHIVES CANADA CATALOGUING IN PUBLICATION
Eriksson, Ann, 1956-   In the hands of Anubis / Ann Eriksson.

ISBN 978-1-897142-35-6

   I. Title.

PS8559.R553I5 2009   C813'.6   C2008-907717-2

LIBRARY OF CONGRESS CONTROL NUMBER: 2008942435

Editor: Lynne Van Luven
Cover images: Top: Raoul Vernede, istockphoto. Bottom: Jan Rihak, istockphoto
Author photo: Lesley Pechter

   Canada Council   Conseil des Arts   Canadian   Patrimoine
                       for the Arts   du Canada   Heritage   canadien

Brindle & Glass is pleased to acknowledge the financial support to its publishing program from the Government of Canada through the Book Publishing Industry Development Program (BPIDP) and the Canada Council for the Arts.

Brindle & Glass is committed to protecting the environment and to the responsible use of natural resources. This book is printed on 100% post-consumer recycled and ancient-forest-friendly paper. For more information, visit www.oldgrowthfree.com.

Brindle & Glass Publishing
www.brindleandglass.com

1 2 3 4 5 12 11 10 09

PRINTED AND BOUND IN CANADA

In memory of my grandmother,
Lavina Spencer, who loved to travel.

Dedicated to my parents.

PROLOGUE
Summer 1966

❦ A hawk drifts high above the shortgrass prairie, rust shoulder feathers lifting over currents of warm air. Below, a figure walks along an overgrown cart track—bare feet, ragged denim cutoffs, the glint of sunlight on a berry pail. The hawk whistles, a thin and descending call.

The young girl squints into the sun to see if the hawk carries prey, but the feathered legs are an empty dark V against the white belly. Summer has painted the child's face and stocky limbs the colour of earth. The two long plaits down her back shimmer with shades of ripened spear grass. Scent of earth and dry weeds wafts into the air and grasshoppers click and leap in flight from her footsteps. Like the rodents and long-legged jack rabbits the hawk seeks, the girl blends with the prairie upon which she walks. In the distance, a log cabin overhangs a coulee where cottonwoods and willows sway. Saskatoon bushes promise her purple-blue berries for evening pie.

"Mind for rattlers, Angela," her mother had warned when she handed the girl the berry pail. Her father had killed a metre-long snake in the haymow Tuesday. She mourns for the reptile and its smooth patterned skin. Like the hawk, she scans the native grassland for movement, ears alert for the slightest sound: an injured killdeer, an orphaned badger or swift fox, a ground squirrel separated from its burrow. She recalls her grandmother's stories of great herds of bison and antelope. The losses, the senseless slaughter. If she lived long ago, she would have offered them sanctuary. No guns, no ploughs. Shortgrass prairie and a young girl to keep them safe.

She descends into the coulee, to the shade of trees and the moist air above moving water. A stream bubbles out of the rocky ground at one end of the ravine and back down at the other. She cools the leathery soles of her feet in the water and searches for frogs, asleep in the muck and wet grass, then settles to her task.

Ripe berries plunk onto the bottom of the galvanized pail, then fall silently. Her hands and mouth grow purple with the warm juice of the fruit. Her head fills again with dreams of her grandparents' old homestead just beyond the coulee: she imagines herself a pioneer with a Red River cart, bumping across the plain, cow tethered behind.

Bucket full, she retraces her steps down the trail, swinging the pail three times in a circle skywards, astonished as always that the berries don't fall in blue rain around her head and shoulders. As she turns for home, a cry stops her in her tracks. She drops the bucket by a clump of sage and runs, ignoring the prickles under her feet, to the cabin yard. A fox kit? A puppy? Or a kitten wandered from a neighbour's farm? The crawl space under the cabin reveals rocks and a rusted hand scythe, a wooden chair with no back, sunlit grasses waving at her from the other side. The cry sounds again from behind the broken chair and she wriggles toward it, oblivious to snakes or the state of her clothes.

A coyote pup is curled in the dirt, head on the ground, chest pumping with the speed of its breath. The whites around its pupils flare and its pointed ears twitch, the velvet of the left ear torn and bloody. Froth foams from the sharp muzzle and a finger-wide gash rakes from neck to shoulder. The smell of clotting blood fills the air. Hawk prey. There might be broken bones.

She reaches her hand toward the pup, which rewards her with a nip, then staggers to its feet and limps away from her into the daylight. She scuttles backwards and when free of the floor joists, races around the cabin to where the pup has fallen onto his side. She kneels and settles her hand on his chest, the heartbeat beneath her sun-browned fingers weedy and rapid. Gathering the limp, matted body into her arms, she turns up the bottom of her T-shirt into a sling and, resisting the temptation to run, heads home. Only when she passes through the gate to the farmyard and sees her brothers tinkering with the engine of the tractor by the barn does she remember the berries.

ONE
Egypt, Winter 1985

❦ Constance Ebenezer stood at the airport window and watched the jetliners taking off and landing, astounded by the ability of the great mechanical raptors to defy gravity and logic. Outside, the German tarmac was as grey and dull as the January sky, but fat wet snowflakes swirled down in spirals and made the scene almost beautiful. The metal birds minded her of the first time she'd ever seen a plane, a day more than sixty years ago when she'd been young and naïve and in love. "Do you remember, Tommy?" she said. "The day you tried to talk me into going up in the biplane?" It hadn't been winter, but spring, and she would never forget the fire in his eyes as they stood in a field of wheat a few miles north of Winnipeg, the fresh green sprouts pushing up through the black soil, the air so clear and hopeful, her hand in his. With his free hand he had traced the path of the biplane across the sky with his finger—the awkward machine banking over the far end of the field—and explained to her how it worked, how the air flowed up and over the wings, causing lift and how the frail-looking contraption could carry them to Lake Winnipeg in half an hour—a trip normally taking the better part of a day on rough gravel roads by car. "We'll be able to see the dunes at Grand Beach and the marshes of Grassy Narrows, maybe even the Icelandic village at Hecla," he had told her, his voice vibrating, so shrill she had wanted to put her hand on his face and calm him. She had tried to imagine the view below, the exhilaration, the wind on their faces, hair whipping out behind them, but the thought of the dizzying height and the reckless speed had only frightened her. She now regretted saying no. He had gone anyway, donning the leather jacket and goggles the pilot gave him, handing the man a five-dollar bill, a week's wages he had earned hauling heavy sledges of building bricks. He kissed her fiercely before he climbed into the passenger's seat. He talked about the experience for months after.

"You wouldn't believe me now, Tommy," she said. "Flying all over the world in planes so big we couldn't have imagined it back then."

Out of the corner of her eye she saw a couple staring at her, then smiling at one another as if they knew something about her that others didn't. She didn't care. She wondered if Tommy had ever gone anywhere in a jetliner. Sadly, she imagined he hadn't ever had the money. She herself hadn't flown in a plane of any kind until at age fifty-nine, twenty years ago now, she boarded an Air Canada flight for Vancouver Island. Rather than going *to* anywhere with intent, she had been running away *from* Donald, so perhaps it didn't really count. But now, she thought with pleasure, flying felt almost old hat.

She picked up her bag, a large canvas carryall her friend Iris had given her for the trip. She hadn't had the heart to tell Iris she found the enormous embroidered sunflowers gaudy, but the bag did the job well enough, although it grew heavier by the day. She also regretted wearing her best skirt suit, which had seemed right the evening before, laid out carefully on the chair in the hotel room downtown. It had been Martin's favourite. And she had been feeling celebratory about her first trip to Africa. Africa! Whenever she thought about it, miniature airplanes in her stomach took flight and she could hardly contain herself. At the moment, though, she was feeling too confined by the close-fitting contours of the jacket and longed for her gardening clothes, the old sweatpants and oversized shirt she'd taken to wearing during the past year since she found herself living alone. She sometimes noted with envy the casual attire of the young travellers in their jeans and sloppy sweaters. The suit would be much too warm for

Nairobi, and she would have to find her hotel and change as soon as she could. Her feet were comfortable though: she looked down and admired the navy and white running shoes she had purchased in Paris a month earlier, after walking the Champs-Élysées and along the Seine for hours in her leather pumps. The blisters on the sides of her baby toes had healed long ago and the cushioned soles of the athletic shoes helped ease the touch of arthritis in her left hip. The store clerk said the shoes were made in Korea.

Constance found a bench and sat down, placing her bag on the floor in front of her feet. According to the woman at the Cairo Air desk, she had several hours before the flight would leave. She had to admit, in spite of the excitement about Africa, that she was feeling tired after six weeks of travelling and sightseeing and different hotels every few nights. She hoped she would be able to sleep on the plane. She leaned forward, opened a clasp on the bag and took out a pen and a post card, a picture of Michelangelo's statue of David from the Uffizi Gallery in Florence, a masterpiece that had kept her in awe for the good part of an afternoon.

Dear Susan, she wrote, then paused and lifted the pen from the paper and her eyes to the ceiling. Whatever could she say to her daughter? *I'm having a lovely time and wish you were here?* She was having a lovely time but she didn't want her daughter here, even though she wouldn't mind some companionship now and then. Susan wouldn't understand what she was doing; she would want her to come home. Constance hadn't been able to write to any of her children. They must be terribly worried, not knowing where she had disappeared to. She turned the postcard back to the photograph of David. "Why on earth, Martin," she said into the air. "did I ever think Susan would like this post card in the first place. She would be horrified and embarrassed by his big stone genitals, wouldn't she?" She could almost see Martin nodding sympathetically, stroking her cheek with his fine slender fingers, then laughing with her at the image of David's jewels. Tears sprang to her eyes. She folded the postcard in half and deposited it in the trash bin beside the bench. This was the sixth post card to Susan she had thrown away. She reached into the bag again, pulled out a magazine and thumbed through it, looking for distraction from her own lonely self, finally settling on an article titled, "Bra Burning to Boardrooms: Feminism in the Eighties."

Trevor Wallace elbowed his way through the line of disembarking passengers. "I have a connection to catch," he mumbled, his new carry-on rumbling behind, a wheeled Samsonite Silhouette suitcase he had given himself as a Christmas present. "Damn," he muttered under his breath as the couple in front of him blocked his way with their slow progress, oblivious to his efforts to pass. Damn the Toronto airport. Damn the weather. Damn the secretary who booked him with such a short changeover. He checked his watch frequently while standing in line at customs, nodding curtly as the officer stamped his passport. He ran for International Departures, almost colliding with a man and his seeing-eye dog. The dog stopped short and gave a single bark as Trevor dodged around them. When he reached the general vicinity for departures, he stopped to check his ticket once more. Cairo Air. *What the hell kind of airline was that?* He'd never heard of it and hoped it wasn't one of those fly-by-night companies that flew bargain-basement planes to questionable destinations. He couldn't believe he had let the office temporary set up this booking without his okay. "I'm too busy right now," he had said. "I'm sure you can handle it. Just make sure I'm in first class."

At moments like this, Trevor wondered how he ever took this job, flying all over the world when he hated airplanes and airports. It was all so difficult: the constant meetings with strangers, an unfamiliar hotel bed night after night, a new situation around every corner. He wished he were home in Calgary, watching hockey in his apartment in Sunnyside, the Bow River flowing predictably outside his door. Trevor liked Calgary, the place too small to be a big city, but more cosmopolitan than Regina where everybody knew everyone else's business. The move from Regina to Calgary over a decade ago had given him distance from Aunt Gladys and Uncle Pat, now both dead, and from the disaster that was his childhood. Trevor loved the river that meandered through the city and had chosen his apartment because of the Bow. The ability to open his curtains at any time of day to see the current riffle and eddy past provided a sense of security. And then there was Angela. He smiled at the thought of the woman he had met the previous winter. He'd just left a Flames game at the newly opened Saddledome and was feeling celebratory after the team's big win. He paused in front of a popular bar, wishing he had a companion to share his excitement. He had pushed open the door and stepped into the noisy, smoky room. The sight of the seething mass of people at the tables, on the dance floor in front of the live band, almost drove him right back out onto the street. As he turned to leave, he caught sight of her on a stool at the bar; her shock of corn-yellow hair drew him across the room. He found himself standing behind her, unsure how to catch her attention. When her friend giggled and gestured with her head toward him, Angela had swivelled around on the stool. Her chocolate eyes grabbed him, shook him gently and set him down as if to say, "Stay still while I tie your shoelaces." When she'd told him over a drink that she practised law, he'd laughed and commented, "No one could ever lie to those eyes."

Life in Calgary was good.

Trevor spotted the sign for *All Other Airlines* across the concourse and picked up his pace. If he couldn't find Cairo

Air there, at least they might be able to give him directions. He glanced at his watch again and as he did so, his left foot connected with something on the floor and he found himself sailing through the air with no time to fling out his arms for protection. He landed so heavily on the granite tile floor that the air was knocked from his lungs and his glasses from his nose. Curling into a ball on his side, he gasped for breath, the world around him obscured beneath a cloak of fog: the river of people parting around him, the benches, the statues, the signs on the walls for duty free and washroom directions. Colours and textures blended together like a child's finger painting, his world transformed into a watercolour wash. He felt around with one hand for his glasses, cringing at the grit on the floor. He would have worn his contacts, but they dried out his eyes on long flights, so he had stowed them in his carry-on with his one pair of underwear, his electric razor and a toothbrush. A hand touched his shoulder and someone placed his glasses in his fingers with a deep *"Ihren brille?"* He put them on. The Frankfurt International Airport instantly came into focus. Rolling onto his back, he looked up to see a patch of sunlight had pushed its way through a hole in the otherwise grey sky. Light streamed in through a high bank of windows above the concourse and illuminated the cavernous space. A head slid into view above him, a face so old and wrinkled he wondered if he were hallucinating, the woman's hair a glowing white aura around her ancient face.

TWO

W The man on the floor reminded Constance of her youngest son, Gregory. Not his features—the hair was darker and curly, the nose larger, the eyebrows finer, the skin paler. But she recognized the innocent bewildered look that came over her son's face at times of stress. It never failed to produce an upwelling of maternal instinct in her. She resisted the urge to gather the man in her arms; instead, she bent down on one knee and took his hand in hers. "Are you all right?" she asked. "I'm so sorry. That was completely my fault."

He shook off her hand and struggled to sit up, almost knocking her backwards on her heels. "I'm fine," he said. "I have to catch my flight." Then a look of panic came over his face. "My bag. Where's my bag?"

"Don't worry." She turned and pointed behind them where the case lay on its side. "It's still here. No one's run off with it. Let's get you up. Can you stand?"

The German who had returned the glasses offered his arm and between them they helped the man to his feet. When the Good Samaritan turned to leave, Constance called after him. "Thank you. *Danke schoen.*" She imagined the poor fellow beside her was too shaken to think of being polite. His clothes were smudged with dirt from the floor, and Constance brushed at a patch on his arm. "You wouldn't imagine such a filthy floor in a country like Germany."

The man stepped back. "Please don't do that. Really I have to go. My plane to Nairobi's leaving any minute." He reached for the handle of his carry-on.

"Flight 2374?" Constance asked, pleased with herself at remem-bering the flight number, her memory for proper nouns and numbers not as good as it used to be. "Cairo Air.

Frankfurt to Nairobi, changing planes in Cairo?"

The man turned to her. "What did you say?"

"Flight 2374. Frankfurt to Nairobi."

But the man wasn't listening. He fumbled in his jacket pocket and retrieved his ticket. He studied the sheaf of papers, then looked up at her as if she had conjured a rabbit from a hat or made a coin disappear and then emerge from behind his left ear. "How did you . . . ?"

"Nothing mysterious. That's my flight too," she assured him. "But you needn't hurry. The plane's been delayed."

"Delayed?" he asked vaguely, as if struggling to understand her.

"At least four hours," she said, enunciating her words and speaking louder in case the fall had damaged his hearing. "A sand storm." She thought for a moment about what the woman at the check-in desk had said, then added, unsure of herself, "or was it a camel on the runway in Cairo?"

He gawked at her, his ticket splayed in his hand and certain to drop to the floor if he didn't attend to it soon. She plucked it from his fingers and slipped it into his jacket pocket. "I'm not sure you are as okay as you think," she said. "Come, sit down. I have to apologize." She wheeled his bag over to the bench where she had been reading about assertive women in business.

He limped after her, brushing down his suit as he walked. She thought he looked taller than Gregory but not as tall as Donald Jr., who was six feet and who towered over her, making him awkward to hug. The man had a slighter build than Donald Jr. too. The thought of her boys, both now men with children of their own, made her think of the house in Winnipeg, then of their father, which she didn't really want to do at the moment. "Can I get you something to drink?"

"No, please," he said. "I need to check in. There might be an earlier flight."

"I asked, there isn't," she assured him. "Please." She shifted over on the bench and patted the seat next to her. "Sit a moment and let me make amends."

A look of defeat came over his face, and to her surprise, he flopped onto the bench beside her. "Amends? For what?" he asked, bending down to rub his shin.

"For your fall," she explained. "You tripped over my bag."

He sat back and sighed. "I wasn't looking where I was going."

"That was obvious," she said. "But the boys get in the way more often than I would like."

"The boys?" He looked around. "Are you travelling with children?"

Constance caught herself. She'd said too much. Iris had warned her not to tell just any old stranger about the boys. "You might get yourself in trouble," her friend had cautioned. So far she'd managed to keep them a secret, but sometimes she wished she could share her adventure with someone. "I haven't even introduced myself." She held out her hand. "Constance Ebenezer."

When he took her hand, she noted that his skin felt as smooth and soft as a young girl's. "Trevor," the man replied. "Trevor Wallace."

Trevor looked down at the hand in his, its spiderweb of wrinkles, the tracing of purple veins under skin as thin as a drape of fine muslin. He'd never held fingers this old, not even his Aunt Gladys's in the years before she died, who'd sooner have strapped his palm than held it in hers. He'd imagined old skin to be cold as if sapped of a vital force possessed only by youth, the texture rough and clammy, and was surprised by the warmth and strength in the woman's grip. Maybe his grandmother had held him with hands this old when he was a baby, but she had died before he was two and he'd never know. He pulled his own hand away and stood. "I'm sorry to be rude but I really need to go. Can you just point me in the direction of Cairo Air?"

"Over there, to the left and around the corner. I'll show you," Constance said and got to her feet.

"No need," Trevor answered, but the woman ignored him and marched across the concourse, the canvas bag bumping against her leg.

The face of the agent behind the counter brightened when she saw Constance. "Mrs. Ebenezer, I hope the wait isn't too tedious?"

"I'm fine, dear. My friend is on the flight too. Could you put him beside me?"

Friend? Trevor raised his hand in protest. "Hold on . . ."

The ticket agent retrieved his ticket and passport from between his fingers and said, "I'll see what I can do," then typed onto the keyboard.

"But . . ."

"Don't worry, Mr. . . . Wallace. Your connection with East Africa Air to Nairobi will be held until your arrival in Cairo." She studied the monitor. "You're booked first class and Mrs. Ebenezer economy. One moment . . ."

"But I—" He looked down at Constance, whose head came only to the middle of his upper arm. All he could see was the fluff of white hair, which he now noticed was faintly tinted with pink.

"Your ticket again please, Mrs. Ebenezer. Normally I wouldn't do this, but . . ." The woman smiled warmly at his companion as if they were old friends. "We have room in first class. I'll bump you up. Any luggage, Mr. Wallace?"

"This carry-on. Wait a minute . . ."

Mrs. Ebenezer turned her face up to him and beamed like a school girl. "Imagine, first class. I'm glad I met you."

When he didn't move, still trying to figure out what to say to reverse the course of the past minute, Constance took his documents from the agent. "You're a Canadian," she exclaimed, fanning his passport in his face. "I should have known." She tucked the papers into Trevor's suit jacket pocket and linked her arm in his. "Thank you, dear," she called out to the agent, and then guided the befuddled Trevor back to the bench. Each time he attempted to speak she interrupted him.

"Do they really serve free cocktails? Not that I drink much, the odd gin and tonic at five before dinner and a nip of scotch before bed. Do you always fly first class?"

She settled her bag between them on the bench and turned a pair of watery blue eyes on him. Her face reminded him of the apple dolls Aunt Gladys made on winter evenings in Regina, the metal-rimmed glasses, the soft hills and hollows of her collapsing cheeks and her scent, like sweet cider mixed with rosewater. She was rambling on about whether or not he knew some people named Wallace from Saskatchewan. Suddenly he wanted to scream.

"Three hours and the whole flight to Nairobi to get acquainted," she carried on, the family from Saskatchewan suddenly forgotten.

A knife of tension drove its way between his shoulder blades.

"Iris worried about me travelling alone, but I told her nonsense, a nice person will come along to keep me company and, well, here you are."

He swore she fluttered her eyelashes at him. *Good grief. She's flirting with me.* "Listen, Mrs. Ebenezer, I—"

"Please call me Constance." She touched his sleeve. "People call me Connie but I prefer Constance. Ebenezer was my second husband's last name. And a scrooge he was too."

He stuffed his anger down into his stomach where it

formed a tight knot. He tried to avoid strangers at all costs. Strangers were too much effort.

"I'm just going to sit over there," he nodded his head toward the next row of benches, "and do some paperwork if you don't mind." He wanted to review the latest company catalogues, memorize the specs on the John Deere 2640 series, although he wasn't sure why he bothered. His boss, Andy, was pressuring him to push their older stock. "Ratchet the price up a bit too," Andy had suggested in spite of Trevor's protest that the new models were more efficient. "They won't know the difference."

"What do you do, dear? Diplomatic service?"

"No."

"A journalist?"

"No, a salesman," he answered sharply. "And I have work to do." Trevor rose to his feet but before he could take a step, the woman pulled him back down by his sleeve.

"You can't possibly concentrate after such a fall," she protested." I'm sorry, I should have taken more care with the boys."

The boys? What the hell did that mean? When his foot hit the bag that sent him flying onto the Frankfurt airport floor, he heard a clunk. No squeak or squeal. And it was solid. Not soft or fleshy. It certainly contained more than knitting. He pointed at the bag and sputtered, in a louder, angrier voice than he intended. "What the hell is in there?"

The expression on her face changed as quickly as the sky over Calgary—surprise, fear, suspicion—each a fleeting ripple across her lined face. She pulled the bag onto her lap, and forehead furrowed, squinted up at him. Her eyebrows were drawn on with pencil.

"So you don't work for customs?"

"No, no. I flew in from Calgary and Toronto." He held up his hands in defence. "Tractors. I sell tractors."

The furrows on her brow dissolved. "Well, that's fine." She relaxed her grip on the handle of her bag. "Useful machines, tractors. Iris insisted I would get in trouble with the boys and that I shouldn't introduce them to any old stranger. But of course you're not a stranger any more." She smiled sweetly. "You're Canadian and I know your name."

Without warning, she plunged one hand into the gaping top of the canvas tote. *What was in there? Drugs?* Trevor resisted the urge to check behind his own shoulder, then watched dubiously as she pulled out an oversize white plastic vitamin bottle—Vitamin C, 500 mg, no preservatives, no artificial colour. Trevor had a smaller one of the same brand in his Calgary apartment. The red hand-printed word on the lid read *Thomas*. She placed the container on the seat between them and without a word, pulled a second from the bag and set it next to the vitamin bottle. Chipmunk Peanut Butter. Commercial size. Crunchy. With salt. All natural. The word *Donald* penned in black on the lid. Lastly, she slipped a sun yellow and brown Magic Baking Powder container, the largest of the three and identified as *Martin* by the neat green block letters on the lid, into the lineup on the bench and sat back. With a flourish of her hand over the three, she announced, "Trevor Wallace. The boys."

Trevor shrugged, puzzled. "I . . . I don't understand. What are these?"

The old woman's eyes glowed with what he could only interpret as pride. "My husbands. My three husbands."

THREE

❦ Constance knew she had gone too far; the poor man looked like Gregory again, perplexed and frightened as a child, cheeks drained of colour. He stared at her as if deciphering hieroglyphics on her face. She put out a hand to steady him, thinking his reaction overstated but aware the announcement was unusual and might sound crazy to most, which is why, up until now, she hadn't told anyone, even customs officers who so far had accepted her explanation that the jars contained herbal powders she needed for her health.

"It's their ashes," she explained, but she expected the news wouldn't really help. The man—Trevor—leaned his elbows on his knees and rested his forehead in his hands. "And not even all their ashes. Only half of them," she added, silently chiding herself for blathering on like a fool. She'd left a portion of Tommy and Martin buried in the garden back home in Sooke, worried at the last minute about the weight of their entire incinerated remains, not to mention finding containers large enough to carry the ashes of a full-grown man. For Donald, she'd received only half in the first place. She settled a hand on Trevor's back, full of regret at her confession. She'd been too hasty, buoyed by the prospect of some companionship for a few hours after weeks of solitary travel. Of course she'd spoken to many people along her journey, but so frequently had felt a language barrier and a sense, an intuition that the time, the person wasn't right. For some reason she had thought she could trust this man. Perhaps she'd been fooled by his nationality, the notion he was from back home. "I'm sorry," she said. "I didn't mean to disturb you."

The day Trevor Wallace turned five and a half, his eight-year-old brother Brent took him behind the silo that rose like a missile out of the Saskatchewan prairie and explained how babies were made. Trevor's father and uncles had spent the day driving combines around the fields while Brent and Trevor rode in the back of the grain truck where the newly threshed kernels spilled in hissing cascades from the combine auger and gathered in soft piles up to their knees. They picked out grasshopper heads from handfuls of grain, then chewed the silky kernels into wheat gum. That evening, while the men washed up and the women laid out a spread of food on two long wooden tables on the west porch, the two boys crouched in the dust and stubble and a patch of black-eyed Susan gone to seed beside the curved metal wall of the silo. Trevor gawked open-mouthed at his brother as Brent described in a hushed voice the basic anatomical details and the result. Trevor's head whirled. He'd been a baby once. Brent too. His mother loved to show them pictures of their first naked minutes on earth. But what made those tiny toes and squashed noses? Surely not this? Trevor didn't know whether to laugh or throw up.

"You're joking me," he said to his brother.

"I read it in a book," Brent assured him. "Honest."

"Swear?"

"Cross my heart and hope to die." Brent drew an invisible X across his chest.

No one would dare to swear a cross on a lie. Young Trevor looked up at the clouds where the pastor from the church down the road said God All the Mighty lived. A picture of God hung in the nave of the church, a furious bearded man, whose watchful eyes knew the very spot where even the smallest sparrow fell. Or the location of the sock of stolen candies in the corner of Trevor's closet. God was not happy when Trevor fought with his brother. He would not be happy to know how babies were made. When the supper bell rang, Trevor crawled out from behind the silo and into a new world of mystery and danger.

Weighed down with the dread of his new-found awareness and unable to eat, he pushed his food listlessly around his plate, watching his parents closely for clues. After his Saturday-night bath where he pondered his floating appendage cautiously, his mother dosed him with cod liver oil, then tucked him into bed and kissed him goodnight. She draped his church clothes neatly over the chair back for morning. After turning out the light and closing the door with a swish of her best dress, she went into the bathroom to dab on a bit of lipstick, then headed to the monthly country dance at the local hall with her husband.

Shortly after midnight, Trevor was woken by the sitter with the news that his parents had died in a fiery head-on collision just ten minutes from the farm. Trevor knew immediately, without a doubt, what had happened. The little boy curled into a ball at the bottom of his bed. Only when Brent slipped in beside him and pulled the covers over their heads, did he allow himself to cry. God All the Mighty had come down from the sky to punish his mother and father for their sins—their two sins, Trevor and Brent.

A childlike jumble of emotions washed over Trevor and left him speechless as Constance made her announcement.

"You look like you're going to throw up, dear," she said. "I didn't kill them if that's what you're thinking. No, it's their ashes. I have their ashes in there."

Trevor, humiliated by the magnitude of his reaction, fought to gain control, while the old woman sat quietly by, the three disturbing containers lined up on the bench between them. He didn't know why, but startling pronouncements had this effect on him, made him shaky and nauseated. He turned his head and focused on her face, her eyes paler than he remembered, so sincere he felt embarrassed.

"It's the jet lag," he finally managed to choke out. "I spent last night on a bench in the Toronto airport."

"I still shouldn't have told you." She reached into the bag again and he cringed, but she merely offered him a bottle of water.

He accepted and eased himself to sitting, unscrewed the top and took a sip. "It's a joke, right?"

Constance shook her head and drew an X across her chest with her index finger. "Cross my heart and hope to die."

Brent's face—he hadn't thought about his brother in years, since the letters started to come back stamped *Address Unknown*—swam like a lazy fish through Trevor's mind, and he shook his head like a dog clearing its ears of water. The urge to run was overwhelming. He resisted, fighting to control his emotions, such dangerous and unpredictable forces. Besides, he suspected flight would land him on his face again, his legs wobbly and untrustworthy.

"Three husbands?" he said in lieu of running. His voice cracked like a pubescent teen's. "In plastic bottles?" He cleared his throat to try to ease the tension in his vocal cords. "You can't be serious." He felt as if he'd stepped into empty space, and the sensation reminded him for a second time of Brent and the day his brother had convinced him to jump from the top of the haystack on the farm. Brent, swaggering and confident on the ground, yelling up to him, "Jump. You can do it." Trevor had looked down from the top, at the golden bales stacked like bricks twelve high, his stomach queasy from the height, and shaken his head, "No." Then suddenly, he'd stepped out into thin air and as he fell, it was as if he were watching himself, amazed at his own audacity, wondering who had made the final choice to jump against his own better judgment. If he remembered correctly, the fall had broken his right arm.

Constance had been prepared for Trevor to walk away; she couldn't blame him after all. She must appear a loopy old woman, and it surprised her when he continued to ask questions. She should lie and admit it was all a silly prank she played on people, a conversation starter, but when she began to tell him that, her heart resisted. The muscles in her chest tightened up and blocked the words welling up from her throat. Her heart wouldn't let her lie to this man.

"I did have three husbands," she said firmly, then laughed at her own words. How they must sound to a stranger. "Not all at once. I hope you didn't think that. No, one at a time."

She watched him closely and was relieved to see the colour seep back into his cheeks. He hadn't dissolved like snow falling into a puddle this time; a slight smile crossed his lips at her confession. She used to be embarrassed that she'd had so many husbands, as if it were an admission of failure, but once they had all died, she quit caring what people thought and now secretly believed it gave her personality a bit of daring colour. "*Ah, I've had only three husbands, dawling*," she would kid around with Iris while having tea on the patio at the cottage in Sooke.

"Shall I tell you about them? How I came to be here with all their ashes?" she asked. "I suppose it must seem crazy."

He nodded his head so very slowly she wasn't sure if he was agreeing that *she* was crazy or the story, but she didn't want to find out. "Which one first?"

He gave a tiny cough in the back of his throat and she suspected he wasn't really taking her seriously. She could understand why, but she was pleased when he pointed noncommittally with his index finger at the Magic Baking Powder container close to his hip.

"That's Martin," she explained.

"He's bigger than the other two," Trevor said.

"Well, I added a few things."

"Added . . . a few things?" His eyes, which she noted were green like Martin's, opened wider.

"In with the body for cremation. His special things. The slippers he wore every evening after dinner, his pipe, his *Complete Works of William Shakespeare*. Those things he loved aside from me. I thought he might need them. You never know."

A half-grin lifted the corner of Trevor's mouth, and she could tell he was trying to suppress a laugh.

"Don't mock me," she scolded and as she shook her head, she could feel the pockets of loose flesh below her eyes tremble above her cheekbones; it was one of the results of aging she had ignored for the longest time and which now added to her annoyance. "Martin's death almost did me in. I loved to have his ashes in the house, to talk to once in a while. We used to talk about everything." She could barely keep the tears at bay and reached into the neck of her blouse for the lace handkerchief she stored in the cup of her bra for convenience.

"Hold on." Trevor held up a hand in self-defence. "I didn't mean to upset you. I'm interested. I really am. Here . . ." He pointed again at the bottles on the bench between them. "That one. Tell me about the one in the peanut butter jar."

She took a breath to still the flapping bird in her chest. She had thought this telling would be simple, that she'd have had time to get used to it all. "Donald," she said shakily. "That one's Donald." A flame of anger flared up, the bird igniting like a phoenix, a reaction she had whenever she talked about her second husband even after two decades of estrangement. "He died a few weeks after Martin," she said, pushing the flame down, telling herself Donald was dead and gone. "I try to keep them apart."

Trevor looked confused. "Apart? Who?"

She paused and considered whether her next statement would have the man carrying her off to the asylum, but it was too late to keep any of it hidden now that she was started.

"Donald and Martin. The idea of the two of them next to one another . . ." She paused and breathed through the constriction that now gripped her throat. "Donald hated Martin." Then she added for clarification in case the man misunderstood, "Martin didn't hate a soul." A single tear slid down her cheek.

Trevor looked away.

Constance blinked, suddenly desperate to regain his attention, as if it were the one thing that would keep her from breaking down completely. "I'm sorry dear, thinking about Martin always makes me a bit weepy." She touched Trevor's knee softly. "He would have loved you." Trevor shifted ever so slightly away from her, and she removed her hand, not wanting him to feel trapped. Intimacy was no good if people didn't feel they had a choice.

She wiped away the tear, sat up and squared her shoulders. Donald was her reality—she couldn't ignore him—so she began again, hesitant, unsure how much to reveal. "Donald died in March—lung cancer." She heard about the death from Susan over the phone, the pain in her daughter's voice, her own odd sensation of freedom. She had refused to fly to Winnipeg for the funeral and spent the day in her garden. She had expected to feel like celebrating but instead found herself crying over her three marriages. Her plan emerged unbidden over the long afternoon, like a seedling pushing its way up through mud into sunlight. "I asked his second wife for a few of his ashes." She paused, recalling how difficult it had been to dial the familiar phone number and hear the woman's voice for the first time on the other end of the line. "I knew he would be cremated, he wouldn't have tolerated the idea of rotting in the ground."

She was aware that Trevor's eyes followed the movement of her hands, two butterflies flitting through the air marking time with her speech, a habit she had never been able to control, even when her father had forced her to sit on them for a half-hour after dinner while he grilled her about her day. "I received a letter from her lawyer demanding a thousand dollars for half of Donald's ashes." She raised her eyebrows. "I always wondered about her motives for marrying him." She wondered if Trevor thought her histrionic. Susan had always complained about her dramatic nature.

"You didn't pay a thousand bucks for them, did you?"

Constance nodded, relieved the young man had finally spoken. "I did."

Trevor studied the squirrel on Donald's peanut butter label. "I guess they arrived."

"Two weeks later. Half of them."

"The better half I hope."

"No such thing with Donald."

Trevor pointed out the remaining container of ashes. "What about this one? Tom?"

"Poor Thomas." Constance answered. She pushed away an overwhelming sadness to concentrate on the living man beside her. "He had nobody." She picked up the Vitamin C container and held it in her lap. "I found him in the obits."

"Obits?"

"The obituaries. The police had discovered his body on East Pender Street in Vancouver and were looking for next of kin." Iris had driven her over to identify him. The police were kind. Over coffee, an officer described the large amount of alcohol found in Thomas's bloodstream, the circumstances of his death. She could only assume the circumstances of his life. They led her into the morgue, slid out a drawer and there he was, a shock to see after so long. An old man, not only dead and stiff, but grey and withered, almost childlike in stature.

"He was homeless," she said. "All he had left were an army knife and a cheap watch."

Trevor sat mute beside her. Had she driven him speechless? "Surprising they would all die in the same year, wasn't it?"

He nodded, but she could see he was groping for words. The airport intercom blared out over the concourse. "Passengers for Cairo Air Flight 2374, please report to the departure desk." The strain lifted from his face at the announcement.

"That's our flight. The sandstorm's over." Constance stood, feeling a sense of relief herself. She couldn't take much more of the memories. She returned her husbands, one by one, to the sunflower bag. "Let's go. We don't want to miss our plane."

"But, you didn't tell me how you got Thomas's ashes," Trevor protested, still sitting in place, looking like Gregory again.

"The police asked me what I wanted to do with him." She jiggled the bag. "And here he is."

She pressed the handle from Trevor's carry-on into his palm. "Come on. We're going to Africa." She headed off. Tiny red lights on the heels of her shoes blinked as she walked.

FOUR

❦ For Trevor, the experience of jet travel fell outside the normal bounds of space and time. The uneasy sense of limitless possibility he felt at takeoff reached a crescendo by the time the plane achieved high altitude. Two shots of scotch, straight up, usually helped, but Cairo Air Flight 2374 was carrying him so far from his predictable well-ordered life that the feeling anything could happen persisted in spite of the scotch. He tried to lose himself in the on-flight magazine, an article about shipping on the Nile, but interruptions from Constance were frequent and persistent as she prattled on about the luxury of first class and the comfort of the leather seats. To his surprise, she matched him one for one on the scotch. Three drinks hadn't made a dent in the speed or coherence of her speech. But most of all, he couldn't get his mind off the three dead men tucked under the seat in front of her. Their morbid presence piqued an uncharacteristic curiosity in him.

"My second husband drank scotch," Constance announced, taking a sip and leaving behind a smear of pink lipstick on the edge of her glass. She looked out the tiny window. "Where do you think we are?"

Trevor craned his neck to see over her head. He could make out green forests and mountains through the intermittent cloud cover.

"The north of Italy?" he guessed.

"Will we miss the Mediterranean? Is it really that wonderful turquoise colour?"

"I've never seen it. But it's getting dark. We'll have to believe the travel magazines."

"You've never seen it? Haven't you travelled every—Oh, listen to me." Constance said. "Inventing stories about you.

Do shut up, Constance. The boy can speak for himself, can't he? Please tell me about your life, dear. I want to know everything." Ice cubes rattled in the bottom of the glass as she drank; her eyes peered expectantly at him over the rim.

Nobody had ever called Trevor *dear* in his life. Uncle Pat's nickname for him was *little shit*. He liked to think his mother might have called him dear, but the possibility had been buried along with her body.

"Well . . . I work for a company called Forrester Agricultural out of Calgary." Why the hell was he telling her this? "We sell farm equip—"

"Donald did his medical residency in Calgary. Donald Jr. was born there." She paused. "Ttsch. There I go again. I'm sorry."

Trevor resumed his explanation with caution, waiting for inter-ruption, but she sat quietly, her eyes intent on his. "I'm the international sales rep." Trevor hated explaining to people what he did. "We have a lot of contracts with foreign aid programs." He paused, wondering if he'd said enough, but she looked on as if expecting more. "I sell tractors to developing countries. Oversee the shipments, stuff like that."

"How noble." Constance sounded impressed. "Helping the poor get ahead. You must feel good about your work," she said.

Trevor shrugged.

"My grandfather had a wonderful old tractor on his farm in southern Manitoba. He treated it like a baby. I think it was called a Massive Harris."

"Massey-Harris?"

"Yes, that's right. Do you sell them?"

He nodded. "We do. They're called Massey-Ferguson now." *But not for long.* There was a rumour the venerable company was in financial difficulty. He didn't think a conversation about the state of the world farm economy would get very far with his companion. He needn't have worried. She changed the subject yet again.

"And you get to travel all the time," she said. "I always wanted to travel. My husbands and I talked about it. But life got in the way and we never did." She nudged the valise under the seat in front of her with her foot. "Until now."

Trevor never thought of his job as noble; it paid the bills. He spent most of his time on planes, in hotel rooms and government offices. Constance acted like she was proud of him. "Yes, exciting," he lied.

"Your wife must find it hard to have you away."

"No, no wife," he said.

"A nice young man like you and you're not married? Girlfriend then?"

Trevor thought of Angela, their occasional lunches and more occasional sex. They had their agreements. Angela wouldn't miss him. "Yes, her name's Angela. She's a lawyer." Trevor loosened his tie and adjusted the air vent. "Well, here comes dinner." He breathed a sigh of relief.

He hadn't eaten a decent meal for hours and wolfed down the casserole, salad and bun. While finishing dessert, he noticed Constance had barely started her meal. He watched as she cut her food into bite-size pieces and chewed each one methodically, nodding her head as if counting to herself, like a sparrow at a feeder, one seed at a time. She washed each morsel down with a swish of chardonnay. She offered him her bun and pudding, which he took, not knowing when the next meal would appear. Once the trays were removed, she laboured over her hands with a napkin, then retrieved the flowered bag from the floor. She transferred the vitamin bottle to her fold-down table and set about brushing it down with a soft bristled whisk from her bag. The name on the lid pulled at Trevor's curiosity. Thomas, husband number one, the homeless man dead on East Pender Street. How did he die? Drug overdose? Mugging? Suicide? He held his tongue, fearing one simple question would bring on another onslaught of incessant chatter.

The cabin lights dimmed and the in-flight movie began. Trevor welcomed the diversion. He fished for his headphones and reclined the seat. An alpine scene appeared on the screen and he fiddled with the controls until music erupted into his ears. The camera panned the smiling face of Julie Andrews, snow-capped peaks in the background. He groaned. *The Sound of Music*. Dubbed in Arabic. With German subtitles. "For Pete's sake," he mumbled, then ripped off the headphones and stuffed them into the seat pocket.

Reaching down a blanket and pillow from the overhead bin, he tilted the seat back to maximum and tucked the blanket under his armpits. Within minutes, the background hum of the jets lulled him into the long slow slide to delicious unconscious. Constance's voice followed him down the hole.

"Thomas was a dreamer. I suppose he died of unrequited dreams."

Trevor couldn't move. His arms and legs were wedged into a narrow passageway. Mucus clogged his nose, and when he opened his mouth to scream—his urge on finding himself in this position—all he could do was mew like a kitten.

Two people—a man and a woman—peered at him from the end of the tunnel. Young—mid-twenties—their faces more work-weary than their years warranted. The man wore a day of whiskers on his chin and a cap emblazoned with the words *Massey-Ferguson*. The brim shaded his face and made it hard to read, but the way he rested his hand on the woman's shoulders gave Trevor the impression of thoughtfulness. The man tapped his knuckles on an invisible wall between Trevor and the couple. The tapping made Trevor blink and when he did so, the woman smiled. In that instant, Trevor knew he had found perfection. Before him hovered the most beautiful creature he had ever laid eyes on. His disabled body relaxed at the woman's gaze and he drank in the details of her features: her honest oval face, the graceful curve of her chin, and the two dimples that smiled from either side of her mouth. Trevor wanted to reach up and touch a dimple. He knew her skin would feel like satin . . . if he could move his hand.

He tried to speak, to ask her to pull him closer, but instead of words, a bubble formed at his lips and broke. The couple laughed again. The beautiful woman brought her fingertips to her lips and the aura of love that radiated toward him made Trevor want to cry.

The man wrapped both arms around the woman from behind and leaned his chin on her shoulder, their cheeks touching. "Well, May," he asked. "What do you think of our new little man?"

"Love at first sight," she said without hesitation. "Love at first sight."

Constance tucked her magazine into the seat-back pocket in front of her and leaned over toward Trevor. The man was tossing about, mumbling things in his sleep, twisted in his blanket. She gently squeezed his arm. "Wake up," Constance said. "You're going to strangle yourself."

Trevor opened his eyes and looked at her out of dazed pupils, then closed them again. Constance tugged at the blanket tangled around his body.

"Let me get you loose," she said. "Got yourself rolled up like a bug in a rug with all your thrashing."

Trevor opened his eyes again only to say, "My mother's name was May," then slipped away once more into half-sleep.

"May's a nice name. You can tell me about her when I have

you back to normal. There." Constance yanked the end of the blanket free.

Trevor struggled to sitting, scrubbed at his face with both hands and squinted into the light. Constance turned off the overhead lamp, which left only the track lights along the floor. Lines of moisture streaked across the outside of the window, and the wing beacon pulsated in the inky night.

"My mouth feels like chalk," Trevor mumbled and pressed his fingers into his forehead.

"Headache?" Constance asked. He nodded. "Bad dream?" The woman arranged the blanket over his knees. "You were mewing like an animal. Going on about love at first sight."

"I don't dream." Trevor searched for a drink, an empty scotch glass with melted ice, anything to quench his thirst. "Excuse me."

"Nonsense, everyone dreams," she said but he was already off down the passageway between the seats, the blanket sliding to the floor in his wake.

Trevor staggered through the door into the washroom. The perfumed urine smell of the cramped cubicle made him want to retch, and his knees nudged the door when he sat on the miniature toilet. He gulped down a dozen paper cones full of water from the tap, ignoring the sign over the sink that read *Not For Drinking*. He threw the last of the water on his face, then leaned his forehead into his palms. Never, ever, as long as he could remember—all his adult life at least—had he had a dream. He was a solid sleeper, his lack of dreams a point of pride. Proof of his clear conscience. Dreams existed for the psychologically unstable, creative types, people with baggage. He massaged his temples with his fingers. But what about the beautiful woman? He saw her. May. And she was gone.

When he slid back into his seat, Constance dropped her

magazine into her lap and draped the blanket over his knees again.

"Listen," Trevor said, "I need to sleep." It was another lie; sleep lived as far away as Calgary.

"Do you?" she asked.

"Do I what?"

"Believe in love at first sight?"

"Now why would you ask me that?" Another topic to avoid. He wasn't sure he even believed in love, let alone *at first sight*. The beautiful woman's face loomed large. He might have loved Brent but he knew that wasn't the love she meant. Besides, he hadn't seen his brother in so long it was a moot point. Neither he nor Angela bought into an arcane notion like love. The idea of love invoked memories of pain. Aunt Gladys said the words once, after she left a wooden spoon bruise on his backside that lasted a month. "It's for your own good. Because I love you."

"You were going on about it in your sleep, dear."

"No, I don't," he mumbled, pulling the blanket up to his chin. "Goodnight."

Constance studied Trevor's face as he burrowed back into his blanket. Maybe he shouldn't sleep again. He didn't look well. She couldn't help thinking that sleeping on planes had a debilitating effect on people. She didn't know if it was the stale air, or the inability to move for long periods, the timelessness, or whether it was the effect of being disconnected from the earth. She never could sleep on planes and always made sure she had plenty of reading material. Trevor had been in some distress, obviously having a nightmare. She herself had been distracted from the magazine article, thinking about Thomas and their short time together.

She leaned over and whispered, "I was thinking about

Thomas when you blurted out 'love at first sight' in your dream."

"Please," Trevor murmured, pulling the blanket higher so it covered his nose. "I'm exhausted."

"I suppose it was really hormones rather than love. I read an article this afternoon about what attracts people to one another."

Trevor didn't respond.

"It can be something as simple as the shape of an ear. Tommy had beautiful ears." She cocked her head and studied Trevor's face. "You have quite nice ears yourself."

Trevor sighed and settled deeper into his chair.

"What did it matter? We didn't last long. How long have you and Angela been together?"

Trevor groaned, unfolded himself from the seat and signalled the passing flight attendant for two more scotches. "Not long," he said.

"Where did you meet?"

He leaned on the armrest, his chin in his hand, and ignored her.

The drinks arrived and Trevor sucked down half the glass in one gulp.

"Thomas and I met in Winnipeg in 1925."

Trevor breathed the alcohol heat out between his teeth. "Bit young weren't you?"

"Nineteen. Old enough."

It had been a grand time in her life. She had finished school and found a job selling housewares at Eaton's on the corner of Portage and Main. She had her own money, and more freedom than she'd ever known.

"I'd get fancied up in beads and flapper dresses, and we'd go out dancing."

"A flapper? Like in the movies?" Trevor asked as if she had told him the world was flat.

Constance imagined it must be hard for him to see her as a young girl, a bob-haired youth in a short baggy dress, high heels, beads swaying as she jitter-bugged across the floor. She'd been quite pretty back then. "I was a regular Louise Brooks."

"Who the hell is Louise Brooks?"

She shook her head and smiled. "Never mind." She didn't bother to tell Trevor how she had to sneak out at night past her father, a process that had been frightening and exhilarating at the same time. She'd been so in love with Thomas that she was prepared to do anything to see him. When her father found out and demanded she break it off, they had run away and been married by a clerk in the city hall in Brandon. She had lied about her age.

"Thomas and I eloped after six weeks," she said. "I thought I might be pregnant."

Trevor visibly cringed. "Another drink?" His voice cracked. He held up his glass. "Good scotch. Do you like it?"

"Not bad, but I still have plenty." She nodded at her own glass, which was half full.

Trevor looked more uncomfortable than ever, so she decided to spare him the details. She'd been so naïve, not pregnant at all, worried that a kiss could make a baby. She was glad modern girls knew more about sex. But her father had been livid. She liked to imagine it was because he'd been cheated out of giving her away, but in her heart she knew it was all about control.

"Are you planning to have children?" she asked Trevor, noting with sympathy how pale his face had turned. The man shook his head.

Perhaps in the end her father had been right. Tommy had disappeared a year later when he lost his job at the rail yard. Who knows where he went? A lumber camp up north, west to the oil fields, Japan on a whaler.

She stared at the back of the seat in front of her, remembering how her father had forced his way into their shabby one-room apartment and taken her home, even though she had been prepared to wait for Tommy for the rest of her life.

"Did you ever see him again?"

"What?" She turned and looked at Trevor, suddenly disoriented, surprised he was there, sitting beside her.

"I mean, after he left. You said he left you."

Constance hadn't been aware that she was talking out loud. "Yes . . . he came back months later looking for me and my father threatened to call the police. I would have gone except for the engagement."

"Engagement? Did I miss something?" Trevor looked puzzled.

"Donald. But that's another story. The point is I let Tommy walk out of my life. My father had the marriage annulled somehow." She smiled and gestured at the white container in her lap. "I like to think this trip repays him for my cowardice and the lost years. Now, tell me about your family."

Trevor shifted in his chair. "A boring story," he said and faked a yawn. "Don't you ever sleep?"

"When you get to my age, every minute counts," she answered. Constance lifted the face of a silver pendant timepiece pinned to her blouse. "It is late." She eased Thomas back into the bag, retrieved her airline blanket from below her seat and draped it across both of their knees. Melancholy enveloped her like fog.

FIVE

§ The tarmac radiated memories of the day's heat as the passengers from Cairo Air Flight 2374 walked through the sultry night air toward the terminal. Constance stooped and deposited her bag on the hard black pavement, then spread her arms to Africa, not sub-Saharan Africa, not yet the deep wild heart of the continent, but still her first steps on its primal soil. "I can't believe we're in Egypt," she exclaimed and threw back her head, breathing in deeply. The air smelled mostly of exhaust fumes and melting tar rather than great herds of animals and wildness.

"Not for long." Trevor stopped and scanned the jetliners parked on the tarmac. "Where's our connecting flight?"

"Must have been a camel on the runway," Constance remarked. She slung her bag into the crook of her arm. "Not a bit of sand about." The scene before her was not what she had anticipated, but she was now an experienced traveller and knew that first impressions were often faulty. She recalled how she had arrived in Amsterdam in the middle of the night on her first flight away from home and been deposited by taxi, exhausted and disoriented, outside her hotel, a decrepit building on a street where women sat half-clad in windows and cafés advertised hashish milkshakes. It had been a shock. But a friendly stranger had directed her to another hotel, which had turned out to be clean and quiet, her room overlooking a canal. By the time she left Amsterdam for Prague a few days later she was completely in love with the city.

She followed Trevor and the straggly line of tired passengers through the double glass doors into the Cairo transit hall, a drab room where sleeping travellers in turbans and robes or jeans and backpacks sprawled on the floor along the wall by the door or crowded the rows of plastic bucket seats in the middle of the terminal. Two officials in khakis stood just inside the entrance behind a cheap metal desk the same colour as their clothes.

"Your passports and tickets please."

Constance and Trevor handed over their documents. The officials studied them, then dropped them on top of a growing pile on the desk. "Please move on."

Constance took several steps then stopped to wait for Trevor who was holding up the line. "Give me my passport back," Trevor demanded.

"My apologies, sir, we cannot," the man explained politely in impeccable English. "While in the transit terminal, all documents must remain in the hands of Egyptian authorities. Please proceed." He pointed to the group of passengers gathered at the other end of the room.

"We're not staying. We're connecting to East Africa Air," Trevor argued.

"With regrets, your flight has left." For the first time, Constance noticed the sidearm on the man's belt. She looked around at the other officials nearby. All wore revolvers on their hips.

"Left? What do you mean left?" Trevor's face had turned red with anger. Constance retraced her steps, took his arm, and whispered. "Let's do as they say, dear."

"Cairo Air said the connection would wait for us." He struggled to loosen his tie, now yelling at the man. "When did it leave?"

"Fifteen minutes ago, sir. Now please. In the dining hall we will explain the procedure for the night." The man turned to the next passenger in line who elbowed in behind Trevor.

"They have guns." Constance whispered into his ear as she steered him toward the other passengers gathering in the corridor. "Let's not upset them."

"But . . ." he protested. "Our flight's gone. Not half an hour ago. How could they do that?" He stared at her as if registering her hand on his arm for the first time. "Guns?"

They joined the crowd waiting along the wall. Constance could hear conservations in both German and English. Everyone appeared exhausted and annoyed at the unexpected delay in their plans. A gentleman in uniform stepped up to the front of the group and raised his hands for silence. "Your attention please. Our apologies. Your flight to Nairobi could wait no longer. You are guests of the Egyptian government. We will put you up in our three-star transit hotel, breakfast included," he announced.

"When's our next flight?" someone called out.

"Our apologies. Your next flight is in one week."

A stunned silence fell over the room.

"One week?" A young woman in tight jeans and sweater fought back tears. "But we've got a safari starting tomorrow. It only lasts a week." Her husband stood beside her nodding, a sleeping child in his arms.

"Why can't we book flights now with another airline?" someone yelled.

"No flights are available," the official answered. A look of annoyance flashed across his face.

"What about our passports?" a skinny German man in a suit yelled.

"Your passports will remain in the possession of customs officials until your departure."

"But we need our passports to go into Cairo, don't we?" another German woman protested.

"You must remain in the transit terminal and the hotel until you leave Egypt. We will be issuing no entry visas. Please, collect your luggage and proceed to the dining hall for room assignments." He swung on his heel, then paused and turned back to the crowd. "Welcome to Egypt."

At his departure, the crowd exploded into a cacophony of noise, like a flock of geese rising from a field. Constance walked over to the window, which looked out over the runway. She couldn't believe her luck. She had regretted not having time in Egypt; it had been one of Thomas's dreams to see the pyramids, walk the Valley of the Kings, sail the Nile, but she'd had to choose between East Africa and Egypt, not having the money for the extra stop. Now fate had intervened. It must be a sign.

Trevor walked up beside her, his glasses in one hand. "How the hell am I going to contact Nairobi and my Calgary office at one-thirty in the morning?" He rubbed the bridge of his nose. "I bet the phones don't work in this godforsaken place. Have you seen any phones?" He looked at Constance. "What are you so happy about?" he growled. "We're stranded in Egypt."

"Exactly." She turned to him with a smile. "Stranded in Egypt."

"Don't look so excited. It's only one night," he said. "Now where's your luggage?" Constance pointed out her large white suitcase on the rack. He grunted as he picked it up. "What do you have in here?" he said. "More husbands?"

"Of course not," she objected, then realized he was joking. "Three was more than enough."

The odour of exotic spices and rancid olive oil hit Constance's nostrils as they entered the dining hall, a long, cheerless room full of wooden tables and chairs, a bar along one wall. Multicoloured tiles in geometric patterns gleamed from beneath a layer of floor dirt, once-grand chandeliers coated in dust hung suspended from the ceiling. Several men armed with clipboards and pens as well as the regulation handgun were arbitrarily assigning people to rooms, men with men, women with women. They paid no attention to the wishes of the passengers, whether married or single, young or old. Several arguments broke out; one German man stalked off to leave his weeping wife in the charge of her new roommates. Trevor leaned against the bar. "I don't care if they bunk me in with King Kong I'm so tired."

Constance hovered at his elbow, suddenly more exhausted than she had been in a long time. In spite of the adventure of the situation, she needed a bed and a familiar face. When the official gestured toward them, she slipped her arm through the crook in Trevor's elbow and when he looked down at her, she stared straight ahead, not wanting to know what he was thinking, not wanting to be alone.

"You . . . and you." The man pointed at Constance and a pair of large sweating Englishwomen at one of the tables. "Room 205." Constance shook her head. The official repeated his order and one of the Englishwomen took Constance's free arm. "Let's do what he says and get a few hours sleep tonight," the woman coaxed tiredly in a broad cockney.

"Constance," Trevor urged. "You're to go with them." Constance tightened her grip on Trevor's arm, thankful when he didn't move or try to shake it off. She was tired of being pushed around by men. Martin had been a dear, always asking her opinion, interested in her ideas, but Donald and even Thomas had acted like she didn't have a brain in her head. The official clamped a hand on her wrist and tried to pull her loose. She conjured up her last ounce of energy, stared him in the eyes and squeezed her fingers tighter.

Trevor grimaced and looked down at Constance. She seemed frail, insubstantial, like a breath of wind could blow her away, and a sympathy rose from a fissure deep in his body like a spray of steam from a crack in the earth. "Get your paws off her," he demanded.

Constance buried her face in Trevor's armpit and began to cry. The official sighed and released her. "Your mother?" he asked Trevor.

Trevor paused, the face of the woman in his dream flaring up in his mind like a twisting flame of fire. When Constance pinched the skin on the inside of his arm, he flinched. "Yeah," he said. "She's my mother."

A barefoot porter, no more than twelve, in soiled trousers and a New York Islanders T-shirt, struggled up three flights of stairs with Constance's large bag. Naked bulbs lit the long empty hallways.

"Three-star hotel?" Trevor snorted. His companion appeared to have recovered and now chattered on to the porter about the weather and his family although the boy appeared to know only a few words of English. By the time they reached their room, she and the boy had become well enough acquainted that she hugged him, then left Trevor to tip him with the few Canadian coins in his pocket. The boy bowed, mumbled something in Arabic and backed away, pointing down the corridor before he scurried off. Trevor dragged Constance's suitcase across the threshold into the room. Inside were a single and a double bed.

"Thank you dear, put my suitcase up here." Constance pointed to the larger of the two beds. Too weary to argue, Trevor heaved the bag onto the mattress. The metal springs squealed in protest.

"Nice room," Trevor said sarcastically as he took in the stained plaster, the single chair identical to the ones in the dining hall and the tacky postcards of Egyptian tourist traps framed on the wall. The red and black tile floor needed sweeping, but he saw no sign of insects and the sheets appeared clean. A high barred window, no glass, framed the black night.

He kicked off his shoes and socks and flopped onto the unclaimed mattress. Constance opened her suitcase and pulled items from it, then turned, a silky nightgown and robe in hand, and cleared her throat. When Trevor didn't respond, she cleared it again.

"What?" Trevor drawled, already half asleep.

"Would you wait in the hall please?" she said. It wasn't a question.

"Oh . . . sure." Trevor sighed, rolled off the bed and stumbled out the door.

Constance closed her eyes, trying to conjure up enough energy from deep inside to get undressed and into bed. Iris insisted that five minutes of deep breathing, a technique she said she learned at yoga, would revitalize anyone, but Constance suspected that Iris, with her long marriage and good health, had never felt such exhaustion as this. But she did try a few long slow breaths and had to admit it gave her a little boost. She undressed slowly, folding her clothes into her suitcase, then slipped into her nightgown and robe, a gift from Martin their last Christmas together. If she'd known what a short time they had left, she would have told Susan and the boys not to visit for the holidays, so she and Martin would have had the brief period alone, in their little cottage with a cozy fire, good books and some wine. There had even been snow on Christmas Eve.

Constance hunted around in her suitcase for her toiletry bag and retrieved a pouch full of pill bottles. She wished she didn't need them, that she could flush them down the toilet, but the wishing only made her wish a hundred other wishes. That Martin was still alive, that people didn't get old and die, that she could reverse time, play God. Then Constance remembered where she was. North Africa. The home of the pharaohs, the pyramids, the Nile. She slid a pill under her tongue and washed it down with a mouthful of water.

Trevor rocked on his heels outside the door, arms folded across his chest, his hands under his armpits. Ten minutes passed. How long did it take a woman to dress? He wandered down the hallway looking for a bathroom and stopped in front of a door marked WC. The sign was unnecessary, the smell unmistakable. The door swung open on a reeking damp concrete room and if it weren't for the painful pressure on his scotch-filled bladder, he would have turned and run. Instead, taking a deep breath, he stepped across the clammy floor. An ancient toilet occupied one corner of the room, the porcelain bowl stained with rust. A broken chain dangled from the wall-mounted tank, which hissed ominously. A rusted showerhead hung precariously in one corner, the floor drain clogged with hair and other detritus. No shower curtain, no toilet paper. He squeezed past the cracked and yellowed pedestal sink to the toilet, catching his distorted reflection in the rippled mirror. He stopped and leaned forward to look at himself. He rubbed his hand across the prickly stubble on his chin. He never went without shaving. Sometimes he shaved twice a day. It would have to wait for morning and the mirror in his bag. He peed into the toilet bowl, then wrapped his hand in the tail of his shirt and yanked on the chain. Water trickled into the bowl. When he turned the tap on the sink, air gasped from the ancient faucet. He scowled at the shower. Likely cold. So far this trip was a disaster.

When he returned to the room, Constance sat on the bed in her nightclothes, a paisley toiletry bag in her lap. "There's no bathroom," she said.

Trevor collapsed on the narrow mattress. "It's down the hall," was all he said and was asleep before she left the room.

Trevor stood alone in an endless field of wheat, arms outstretched. The stalks reached to his waist and the feathery heads, heavy with grain, brushed against his open palms. Overhead a cloudless robin's egg sky. Swallows flitted past and the rasp of crickets rose from the ground near his feet. Heat from an invisible sun settled onto his head and shoulders like a blanket.

At the horizon, the pristine landscape was suddenly interrupted by dark shadows of falling grain. Swaths of wheat cascaded toward him like waves onto a beach. A tractor burst over the crest of the hill. An American-built Steiger Panther four-wheel drive. One of the biggest tractors made. Its huge knobbly tires turned through the field, knocked over fragile stalks, ripped out roots. The wide brim of a Stetson hid the driver's face from view. The huge machine circled around Trevor, leaving him stranded on an island of gold. He closed his hands around the hot seed heads, which crumbled between his fingers as he sank to his armpits in scorching sand. Without warning, the tractor transformed into a red convertible spinning three-sixties in the desert. The chrome bumper flashed in the sun. The driver's hat blew into the field and Trevor recognized the man's face: his father. May sat next to him, smiling broadly, eyes bright. The pair waved as they circled. He called out but they drove away, laughing, the car fishtailing through the desert. Sand flew in sheets from behind the tires. Music drifted toward Trevor from their radio, distant and indiscernible, growing louder until it surrounded him, demanding and foreign.

Constance slipped from her bed and padded barefoot across the room to the high narrow window, quietly carrying the chair from the corner to the wall, and climbed up, having to stand on her tiptoes to see out. She breathed in the scent of tropical flowers she didn't know the names of and listened to the muezzin call wafting through the window bars. Outside, the moon hung like a silver scimitar in the inky sky that unfolded across the desert beyond the buildings, the lights of Cairo a distant glowing canopy over the city. In the streets below, people walked toward the mosque under the sickly yellow cast of the streetlight. The haunting chant drew them like bees to honey, the honey of their lives, their religion. While she admired their devotion, she'd never been willing to embrace any religion wholeheartedly. Donald had insisted they take the children to church every Sunday, but during the week he was horrid. It all felt so hypocritical, living life as if their religion didn't matter. She wished Tommy were here, with his own special religion, his passion for life. She'd never met anyone who loved life more, not even Martin.

Trevor stirred in his bed. She hadn't wanted to wake him, hoarding this moment for herself. "Constance?" his sleepy voice called out. She didn't answer, hoping he would drop off back to sleep, but instead she heard him groping around on the table beside the bed for something—his glasses maybe—which fell to the floor with a clatter. As he stumbled across the tiles to her bed, he mumbled something about "fucking dreams." She imagined with regret he would find her wig hanging on the bedpost and she had her hand on her head when he crept across the floor toward her, his clothes creased with wrinkles. She must look a fright, white nightgown gleaming in the moonlight like a ghost. She gripped the bars with her free hand. As he drew nearer, she could tell from the puzzlement on his face that he had noticed her hair, the wispy tufts and patches of down, the pink scalp peeking through. Bless his heart, he said nothing, only whispered, "What are you doing?"

She pivoted on her toes, lowered her heels to the chair and dropped her hand from her head. "It's the call to prayer," she whispered and beckoned to him, "The call of the muezzin." She turned back to the window. "Isn't it marvellous?"

Trevor grimaced as he crossed the cold gritty floor. He

leaned against the wall beside her and together they looked out over the broad concrete window ledge. The landscape below was a sea of flat rooftops and whitewashed buildings. Dim orange streetlights illuminated a narrow paved street below. A truck snaked along the road, people crowded onto the flatbed. A cloaked form appeared in a roof garden not far from them and bowed, arms outstretched.

"What's happening?" Trevor asked.

"The Islamic Call to Prayer," Constance whispered. "They pray five times a day to Mecca. Thomas would have loved this."

"Mecca?" he whispered back. "Why are we whispering?"

"The holy city of Islam. In Saudi Arabia. Muslims believe it's the original place created on earth."

"Everybody prays five times a day?"

"Everybody who's devout Muslim." She turned to him, the shadows on his face eerie in the moon glow. "You've never seen this before?"

"Oh . . . sure . . . just not in the middle of the night," he mumbled. "I'm not religious."

She knew he was lying to her. Why not? She was merely a stranger he would never see again. For some reason the thought made her sad.

"I'm going back to bed." Trevor pushed away from the wall.

Constance felt a smidgen of guilt at the unbridled annoyance in his voice. She watched him stumble back to his bed. This time he stripped down to his underwear before rolling onto the mattress. A sudden longing to feel a warm body next to hers again washed over her as he turned onto his side and pulled the thin sheet over his shoulders. She'd been alone too long.

She turned back to the window and watched until the truck disappeared around a corner and the sounds faded into the night.

SIX

◗ "Hissss." Trevor shooed another scrawny cat off the table. A half-dozen emaciated flea-bitten felines roamed the dining room. He wasn't surprised; the rest of the place—the utensils and dishes, the floors, the windows onto the runway and the boring desert—needed cleaning. At least the coffee had bite.

A grey tabby prowled around under their table, yowling with hunger. The animal was in luck today, Constance fed it a triangle of flatbread slathered with yogurt and honey. "Don't be hard on the cats, they rely on us for food. I've got three Siamese at home. Mind you, they aren't allowed on the table in my house." She stroked the cat's back. It arched and purred, hipbones jutting through its dull coat. "Poor thing."

"That Englishwoman from last night told me she heard the Egyptians lie to air passengers to keep them here as tourists," Trevor said.

Outside the dining hall window, a row of jets lined the tarmac. He knew one of them must be Nairobi bound. Even at 8 AM, heat rose off the asphalt in shifting waves. Armed guards lounged near each plane and at every airport door or gate. Trevor pressed the heels of his hands against his forehead, a headache raging again.

"How the hell will we get out of here?" he grumbled.

He'd tried to call Nairobi and Calgary from the phone at the front desk—the one phone in the entire transit area of the airport—which rewarded him with a jumble of unintelligible Arabic followed by a dial tone. He couldn't even send a telegram. Through the dining-room doors he watched their fellow passengers in the transit hall lobby pound on the desk, insisting on passage to Nairobi.

"We apologize. Your next flight departs in one week. Please enjoy your stay," Trevor said, mocking the infuriating official to whom he'd spoken twice.

A man in a three-piece suit, hair slicked back and shiny, worked the crowd with an invitation for a bus tour to his uncle's perfume shop. Compliments of Cairo Air and the Egyptian government. Chaperoned by armed guards, Trevor imagined. Uncle Faisel's perfume store, Auntie Tutu's tea shop, the family carpet factory. Drop your money here.

"And are you enjoying your stay in Egypt?" Trevor said to Constance who was whisking ants out of the sugar bowl.

"Don't be sarcastic, dear. Our stay has just begun," she said, looking up at him.

"Are you signed up for the bus tour?"

"Not today. I have other plans for us." She handed him a small glass bottle from her bag. "Take two of these and don't drink any more coffee. I'll be right back."

Trevor picked up the bottle. Aspirin. How did she know he had a headache? She disappeared up the stairs to the room. What the hell was she up to? He signalled to the waiter for more coffee.

Trevor hadn't touched the coffee by the time Constance returned a half-hour later. Her wig was freshly coiffed and she wore a flowered dress with a round white collar. Except for the running shoes, she looked like she was ready for church.

"My granny dress," she confided, brushing out a wrinkle in the skirt. "I thought it might come in handy."

She'd made herself up in eye shadow, a hint of blush on each cheek and a careful line of pink lipstick. Milky pearl earrings dangled from her earlobes. She held a white leather purse in one hand, the canvas bag of husbands in the other, which she deposited on the table in front of Trevor. "Would you hold the boys, please? We wouldn't want them to get in the way again."

When she whirled around and marched across the dining room and into the lobby. Trevor grabbed the bag and jumped up—the boys weighed more than he had imagined—and followed. Constance strode into the transit hall and up to a nondescript door guarded by a young soldier who jumped from his chair as she approached. She lifted her chin and spoke to the man, who didn't move, speak or react in any way, his eyes fixed straight ahead on a distant invisible object. Trevor stopped twenty steps away and eyeballed the man's shiny weapon, the one clean thing he'd noticed since arriving in Cairo. Constance looped her purse over her arm, eased her hand under the guard's armpit and knocked on the door. When the door swung open, the old woman exchanged words with someone inside. The sentry stepped aside and she disappeared through the doorway. The door shut behind her with a click.

As Constance vanished, emotion dug its talons into Trevor's throat. This disturbed him, for he prided himself on his ability to keep emotions at bay, all emotions, pleasant and unpleasant. Rampant emotion was dangerous, and responsible for most of the ills in the world. But this feeling, not rampant, but indefinable, left Trevor at a loss. Constance was out of sight and therefore uncontrollable, and had left him with three dead men in a sunflower carryall. What if she didn't come back?

He looked down at the bag in his hand—for all he knew the ashes were flour— and let it slip to the floor. He didn't have to wait, he told himself. After all, she was a mere stranger, a madcap woman with a madcap story. Tomorrow she'd be history. Trevor turned and walked swiftly through the hotel lobby and up the stairs, jumping from one step to the next with the relief of his decision. By the fourth step he slowed and by the sixth he stopped. He turned until he could see the bag, slumped against the wall across the room where he had left it, forlorn as an abandoned child. "Damn," he muttered, then kicked the seventh step and returned to the transit hall.

Trevor leaned against the wall—Martin, Thomas and Donald at his feet—and waited, arms folded, chewing on his lip while he assessed the situation. Constance had disappeared behind the nondescript door ten minutes ago. The soldier appeared no less fierce and immovable, his gun no mirage. Why hadn't she come out? A spot in the middle of his chest responded to the question with a twinge. He rubbed his index finger on a grease stain on the front of his sleep-crumpled shirt. Undeniable. He felt this twinge every time he took on a new sales job. Responsibility. But never, never in his life had this feeling, this emotion—he winced at the word—translated to another human being. He should go after her, he knew, but the soldier at the door, a boy of eighteen or twenty, looked foolish, as if he wouldn't hesitate to use the gun if provoked, taking pleasure in target practice on a foreigner. Trevor looked in the direction of the desk where the crowd of delayed passengers milled, arguing with the Cairo Air staff, and felt a measure of comfort knowing he had a noisy insurance policy and witnesses. The Egyptians wouldn't relish an international incident involving tourists.

He swallowed hard and stepped resolutely forward. The guard didn't move, but Trevor was sure the fellow's hand tightened on the barrel of the gun. Heart pounding, he took three more steps, each with increased confidence, and rehearsed a small speech under his breath, debating on the tone of his argument, whether demanding or apologetic, when the door opened, the soldier stepped aside and Constance emerged, smiling. She patted the sentry's trigger hand. As she swept past Trevor, she leaned over and whispered, "Shall we get our things before they change their minds?"

"What was that all about?" Trevor trailed her up the stairs

toward their room. "Who were you talking to? Did you know you could have gotten yourself in big trouble? Those men have guns. They are insane. Would you tell me what's going on?"

Once in their room, Constance locked the door and sat on the bed.

"Well, are you going to fill me in?" he demanded.

Constance opened her purse and held it out to Trevor. Inside, neatly bundled, lay their passports and tickets.

"Where . . . how?" He gawked at the documents.

She smiled sweetly.

"Everyone has a grandmother."

SEVEN

◈ The cool air and subdued light of the Egyptian Museum was a relief after the brilliance of the noon sun outside. Trevor studied a tray of long metal hooks mounted in a glass box. The sign below explained the instruments were used to extract the brain of a corpse through its nostrils as the first step in the embalming and mummification process. Trevor grimaced and rubbed his nose with his index finger. Did Constance know about mummification before she settled on ashes? At the other end of the room, she was bent over the contents of a display case, talking to herself, likely a lecture to the boys—secured in their bag under an elbow—on the history of Egypt. She had insisted on leaving her suitcase in the waiting cab, the driver happy to sleep in the sun for American dollars, but Trevor had refused to leave his luggage with the dubious character. His arm ached from manoeuvring his carry-on through the narrow corridors of the museum.

A gilded wooden statue of an animal next to the case of hooks caught Trevor's attention. He studied the ebony head, trying to determine what kind of animal it was, the long sharp muzzle and upright ears reminiscent of a fox or a prairie coyote. According to the caption, modern-day Egyptians didn't know what kind of animal it was either, likely a jackal or a wild dog, animals which haunted the edges of the desert where the dead were buried. The statue, which had been discovered at the entrance to the tomb of King Tut-ankh-amun, symbolized Anubis, the canid-headed God of Embalming, guide and protector of the dead through the underworld to the afterlife. A carving on stone beside the statue depicted the same god as a man with the head of a dog. He stood upright on two human legs, staff in one hand, the other hand outstretched. Trevor read the description.

> The canid-headed Anubis (uh-noo'-bis), also known as "He
> Who Counts the Hearts," steadies the scales on which the
> heart of the dead is measured against the feather of Ma'at. If
> the heart is light as the feather, Anubis guides the soul to the
> afterlife, the Kingdom of Osiris; if found to be heavier, the
> heart is fed to the god Am'mit and the soul destroyed forever.

Trevor shook off the dark cloak of dread that descended
on his shoulders as he read. Why were people obsessed with
death? He hadn't given it much thought. *You were here one
day, gone the next.* Who cared what happened to a body after
death? As far as he was concerned, the ancient Egyptians had
practised the ultimate in self-deception, stuffing tombs with
gold and jewels to use in another life, pickling themselves
in vinegar and strips of cloth, all so a man with an animal
head could escort them to another life. He reached down and
traced the shape of the god on the plaque. *If you were lucky and
your heart didn't weigh more than a feather.*

He shivered, suddenly feeling cold. He looked around for
the source of the unexpected shift in temperature. An open
door to an underground crypt? A ceiling fan? The state of this
famous museum surprised him. The walls were rough and
unadorned, the floors crisscrossed with dusty footprints as if
he and Constance were the lone visitors in a decade. Piles of
unlabelled artefacts difficult to describe as exhibits crowded
the shelves and tables. It felt as if they had stumbled into
a storeroom instead of the real museum. But he had seen no
armed guards, which was a comfort.

Once they had escaped the airport transit hall with their
luggage and travel documents, his goal had been to find the
East Africa Air desk to inquire about flights to Nairobi, but
somehow Constance had bewitched him, talking him into a

few hours in Cairo. First the Grand Bazaar, a crowded noisy maze of alleys and rickety kiosks that reeked of spices and dead chickens. Street urchins pulled at their sleeves to offer them slim glass mugs of sweet, milky tea; vendors hawked flat-bread and sheep cheese, cheap sunglasses and rubber thongs. While Constance bought almost everything shoved in her face, he refused the pleas and taunts of the begging crowd and guarded his back, his hand jammed into his front pants pocket to protect his wallet.

At least the museum was quiet. Had she said she needed his protection? He didn't recall those exact words. He should be on a plane instead of wandering bored through the musty remnants of ancient Egypt.

"Trevor, come and see this." Constance gestured to him from across the room with her free arm, the other taken up by husbands. He felt like the fourth victim going to slaughter. Did she have an iron hook tucked in the bag with the boys?

Constance watched Trevor thread his way between the table and display cases. His face looked particularly pinched and unhappy, and she felt a twinge of remorse at talking him into accompanying her to the museum. Next to Donald, he was one of the most uptight people she'd ever met. She wondered about his childhood, his life at home in Calgary, which he had so far been reluctant to discuss. She appreciated the little rifts in his façade that opened up when he was pressed, providing glimpses of a gentleness that wasn't otherwise apparent. She'd been particularly relieved to find him waiting with her bag when she emerged from the airport office with their passports. Earlier, when he'd lied and said she was his mother, she could have hugged him.

"Who's this?" Trevor indicated the horizontal lit glass case where an ornate form lay on black velvet.

"The Boy King. Isn't it marvellous?"

The simple sign on the end of the display read *King Tut-ankh-amuns's Death Mask-1350 B.C.*, the mask solid gold inlaid with lapis lazuli and glass.

"Not bad," he said. "No dust. Another of your husbands?"

"You're naughty. It's King Tut, his burial mask, one of Egypt's greatest treasures," she scolded. She regretted that Thomas wasn't here to see King Tut. He'd dreamed about travelling to Egypt, a fleeting dream like all the rest. He'd come home one afternoon, arms loaded down with every book on Egypt he could find in the Winnipeg library. They spent the afternoon on the floor of their one-room apartment while he showed her picture after picture of pharaohs and tombs and gods with strange names and special attributes.

"I think that's his dog over there," Trevor pointed his thumb behind him.

"Dog?"

"Well, a guy with a dog's head they found in his tomb."

"Anubis?" Constance's eyes lit up. "He was one of Thomas's favourites. Show me."

Trevor led her over to the statue.

"Oh, lovely," she said, admiring the smooth graceful lines of the canine. "Thomas thought Anubis was one of the most important figures in Egyptian culture. Just like it says here." She read the inscription. "The ultimate guide and protector for the soul on its journey to heaven. Without Anubis, you'd wander around in the underworld forever. How awful."

"Might be better to be devoured by Am'mit. Imagine what he's like," Trevor teased. "So Tom was an expert on Egypt in addition to his other talents?"

"He dreamed of being an Egyptologist."

"Obsessed with death too, was he?"

"Oh no, the opposite. Obsessed with life. With eternal life." Constance bowed closer to the plaque to examine the details of the drawing of Anubis in his man/canine form with its black pointed muzzle, upright ears and glowing eyes. "Haven't you ever thought about life after death?"

Trevor sighed. "Can't say I see any point in it. I haven't heard much convincing evidence there's more than this." He waved his arm vaguely through the air, then leaned against the dusty display table behind him, and crossed his arms.

Constance turned to him. His face was as impenetrable as a stone wall. "But the soul, Trevor, what about the soul?"

He shrugged.

"It doesn't matter, dear." She placed her hand on his arm. "I have one more place I want to go before the airport." She turned and headed down the corridor to the exit. Trevor hurried behind, his carry-on bumping against his hip.

"At least you could tell me where we're going," he called after her.

To Trevor's surprise, the taxi hadn't left. The driver lay sprawled across the front seat, feet out the open window, cap pulled down over his face, waking only when they opened the door.

"The Great Pyramid, please." Constance said.

In spite of his increasing annoyance at the way the old woman took it for granted she could lead him around like a dog on a leash, Trevor's ears perked up at the mention of the pyramids, one place even he could get excited about. He recalled building a model of a pyramid in grade school out of hundreds of tiny white sugar cubes, mystified at how the Egyptians had constructed them without power tools and huge machinery. His pyramid had fallen over, the cubes spilling across the desk like an avalanche of snow.

The driver steered the car into the chaos of the ten-lane throng of vehicles, motorbikes and donkey carts, where the traffic ignored the signal lights and pedestrians streamed like water through the gridlock. A woman robed in black from head to toe carried a heavy cabinet on her back across the road in front of the taxi. She fixed her gaze on Trevor through a narrow slit in the cloak. He shifted in his seat at the intensity of her scrutiny. Her head swivelled to maintain her visual grip on him until she reached the sidewalk. The temperature had risen since they set out; he rolled up his sleeves and loosened another button on his shirt, then closed the window against the stench of exhaust.

The taxi sped along a broad palm-lined avenue that followed the muddy Nile where traditional feluccas, with their graceful lateen-rigged sails, tacked between steel barges and modern cruise ships. They left the green ribbon of vegetation along the path of the river, and headed into the desert. Trevor expected signs of habitation to fall away as the land grew more desperate, but on both sides of the road, whitewashed mud brick houses jumbled together and spread across the monotonous colourless landscape, more barren than the Saskatchewan prairie where he had grown up. He had always imagined the desert as ephemeral hills of drifting sand reminiscent of rippling fields of wheat, but the ground here was ugly and dull, rough with rubble.

"Godforsaken place," he hissed under his breath. Then aloud. "Do you have air conditioning?"

The driver shook his head. Constance fanned her museum program in front of her face. She had changed clothes before they left the airport hotel and now wore khaki slacks, a white sleeveless blouse and a broad-brimmed straw hat. Trevor understood why her suitcase weighed a ton, an outfit for every occasion. All he had were his single pair of polyester suit pants and his one shirt, which stuck to his back in the forty-degree heat. Ahead the three massive pyramids at Giza soared above the flat housetops.

Constance stopped fanning, leaned forward against the front seat and peered out the window. "My friend Iris says people who climb the pyramid have the irresistible urge to jump off when they near the top," she announced.

"How would she know that?" Trevor leaned back, a now familiar knife of tension lodged between his shoulder blades.

"Iris reads a lot," Constance answered. "Do you like to read?"

But Trevor had closed his eyes, feigning sleep, and didn't answer. He wondered if she knew he was faking.

"The ancient Egyptians believed the afterlife was a continuation of their existence on earth. However, the reasons for building these huge pyramids remain a mystery to Egyptologists. We know only that they housed the vestiges of the Egyptian royalty, the pharaohs and their wives. This particular pyramid, known as the Great Pyramid, is the largest of all the Egyptian pyramids and the tomb of the ruler Khufu, also known as Cheops. The structure is considered one of the Seven Wonders of the World. It rises 150 metres and contains 6.5 million tons of limestone. Each block weighs . . ."

Trevor opened a few more buttons on his shirt and mopped his forehead with his shirt sleeve, but the wind and the desiccating heat sucked every drop of moisture from his skin and blew it off into the desert. A whirlwind of sand twisted through the crowd of tourists as they listened to their guide lecture about the pyramids. Trevor brushed the grit from his eyes with the back of his hand. Off to their left, two Arabs in flowing robes lounged astride camels, long colourful pompoms and bells dangling from the animals' bridles and saddles, their gawky heads lifted into the wind, thick fleshy lips open to reveal worn square teeth yellow with age. One hump. A hand-drawn sign—*Camel ride $25 American dollars*—hung from the back of the saddle. Anything for a buck. He'd heard the damn things spit in your eye if you got too close. Behind the camels rose the bulk of the Sphinx, its face encased in scaffolding, nose missing. According to their guide, it had been blown off by Turks during target practice. Like the transit hall airport, the pyramid grounds crawled with armed guards.

At his elbow, Constance concentrated on the lecture, her chin tilted upward with interest. Except for the pink flush on her face from the heat and the coating of cinnamon-coloured dust on her runners, she appeared as cool and collected as if on a shopping trip in a Canadian mall. How could she wear that wig in this heat? Trevor checked his watch for the twentieth time. The pyramids were nice, but after five hours of sightseeing, it was time to get back to the airport and hunt down a flight to Nairobi. A pariah dog sniffed at his shoe, and he kicked it away.

The tour group moved en masse toward the pyramid entrance. He'd made up his mind: this was his last concession to Constance. He'd done his bit for Egyptian tourism. If she refused to go with him, he'd damn well leave her.

"Would you hold the boys for a moment?" Constance slung the flowered bag onto his wrist. "I need to find the little girls' room."

"You mean you're not going in there?" He gestured toward the low dark opening to the pyramid, feeling at last a glimmer of possibility.

"I wouldn't miss it for the world. You go ahead. I'll catch up." She hurried away toward the ticket building.

"Do you know your way?" he called. "How will you find us? Constance!" Another mini whirlwind swirled into his face. When he recovered, she was nowhere to be seen.

He filed through the squat dark doorway into the bowels of the pyramid, hitting his head on the overhead limestone block. A narrow tunnel, lit with weak electric lamps set into recesses in the walls, angled upwards. He followed the passageway and the legs in front of him. The air was close and musty. He struggled for breath, heart pounding. Cold sweat stained his armpits. He had hated enclosed spaces since he was twelve, when Uncle Pat locked him in a closet for a D in math. He turned and looked behind him. Where was Constance? Should he wait for her? The man behind him scowled and shuffled his feet impatiently. Trevor gripped the metal railing and continued, stooping as the incline steepened and the roof sloped downward. The tunnel closed in on him. He strained to hear the guide at the front of the line: a caution about the need to crawl to reach the king's chamber.

Forty-five minutes later, Trevor emerged into oven temperatures and the blinding light of the desert afternoon, thankful for liberation from the claustrophobic interior of the pyramid. Why hadn't Constance returned to the group? He wanted to share some facts gleaned from the tour. That like her, the ancient Egyptians also buried slippers and books with their loved ones—well not slippers and books—but things they might need in the afterlife: jugs of oil and expensive jewelled crowns, even mummified dogs. He grinned at a vision of Martin, atop a cloud, absorbed in the *Complete Works of William Shakespeare*, sucking on his pipe and wearing his favourite slippers, little wings folded on his back.

Someone ahead shouted and pointed at the pyramid. The group of people in front of him stopped and turned. A wave of excitement rippled through the crowd. A gunshot rang out. Trevor lifted his head and looked too. Two-thirds of the way up the face of the pyramid, someone laboured from stone to stone, a second person in pursuit several levels below. Guards milled about the base of the pyramid, gesturing and yelling in Arabic.

"A climber," a man ahead of Trevor announced to his wife. Both were dressed in red and green plaid Bermuda shorts and T-shirts that bore the logo Pharoah Tours. A spider's web of cameras, binoculars and sunglasses hung around their necks.

"A man died last week, fell right from the top," the woman said, eyes shaded from the sun with an upturned hand.

Trevor carried on toward the parking lot to look for Constance. He hated the way people gravitated to drama and gawked in crowds, feeding on one another's lust for blood. He expected they would soon start chanting "Jump, jump." Barbarians. He stopped and turned in a circle. Where the hell had Constance got to? He wanted to get out of here, and she had left him with her bag yet again. Had she been distracted by a camel or another chance meeting? He wiped his knuckles against his parched lips and checked the canvas carryall for water: whisk brush, two husbands, no water. *Two* husbands? He whirled around and squinted up at the figure scaling the last levels of the pyramid, then ran back to the crowd and grabbed the arm of the American in the Bermuda shorts.

"I need your binoculars," he yelled.

The man stepped back, startled.

"Now!" Trevor bellowed, seized the binoculars from around the astonished tourist's neck, and shoved the eyepieces against his face. He fumbled with the focus, then sucked in his breath as the scene became clear.

"Oh, my God," he mumbled under his breath.

Constance did not dare look down. At first, she had been afraid the blocks of stone would be too large, too smooth from centuries of wear and weather to climb, but she needn't have worried about that, there were plenty of hand- and footholds. The problem was that she could already feel the pull of the pyramid, just as Iris had said. The urge to leap off into space, or perhaps it was merely gravity, drew her attention back to the ground, where she suspected she ought to be. The impulse to climb the pyramid with Thomas, who hung in a plastic bag from her belt, had formed in her head only minutes ago as she listened to the tour guide talk about the dimensions of the structure and its illustrious past.

Gregory had a fear of heights as a child. She had been forced to hold his hand whenever they crossed the bridge over the Red River near their home, the poor boy in tears the entire span, unable even to look down at the boats on the river, something he normally loved to see. But it wasn't acrophobia that kept her from looking down, it was the fear she wouldn't be able to make it to the top. She looked up at the pinnacle of the pyramid, the hot white sky beyond. What if she didn't reach her goal? Thomas, the master of lost dreams, was counting on her.

She could hear the young Egyptian below, the crash of falling rubble dislodged by his boots, his wheezing breath; she expected he was a smoker like most of the young men she had seen so far in Cairo. Donald had smoked, a filthy habit she abhorred. She despised the dirty ashtrays around the house, the stink on his clothes, the foul taste in his mouth when he kissed her. Even when Susan had asthma as a baby, she couldn't get him to stop. In the end cigarettes had done him in. She felt a jab of self-righteousness, and then was instantly ashamed of herself.

The sign had been obvious, in five different languages. *Climbing of the Pyramids is Prohibited.* Normally, she abided by laws and regulations, but since Martin died, she had found herself crossing the street against the light. Or even jaywalking. Once she took a keychain from the drugstore in Sooke even though she didn't need it. When she confessed her transgression to Iris, her friend had laughed. "You're almost eighty and you're finally rebelling. Has being good all your life really helped?" Maybe Iris was right. So far her little insurrections hadn't turned her into a bank robber or a murderer.

The wind grew stronger as she climbed; she was grateful for the fitness classes she and Iris had attended at the community recreation centre. Even so, she had to stop occasionally to catch her breath, ever conscious of the progress of the guard behind her. "Stop," he called out to her in rasping English every few minutes.

The top could not be far, but it was difficult to tell. When she looked up, the desert sun blinded her. She blinked, her vision marred by dark patches left by the glare. She tried to ignore how tired she felt at each handhold, every foothold. One step at a time. She concentrated on the patterns in the limestone and marvelled at how the stone had once been an ancient seabed. How strange it was that it now stood in the middle of a desert.

In the instant the image of the ancient seabed came to her, she realized she wasn't going to make it. It wasn't just the proximity of her pursuer and the exhaustion. Suddenly it didn't matter whether she was on the top of a pyramid, or at the bottom of the sea. She had done Thomas justice. She, his Constance, had dared to fly.

With a last heroic effort, she heaved herself onto the next slab of rock. Her back protested as she steadied herself and struggled to a standing position. Her pant legs fluttered in the wind. Her hands shook as she untied the plastic bag from her belt and retrieved the vitamin bottle. She unscrewed the lid and held Thomas up to the infinite sky.

The American tugged at Trevor's arm. "Give me my binos, you thief." His wife complained loudly in the background. Trevor ignored them both, his attention fixed on Constance, who appeared to be stalled on a bench not three levels from the top, the guard not far behind. All around him people cheered her on. "She's going to make it." "Keep going." "Don't stop now."

Through the binoculars he watched Constance stagger to her feet and raise her arm. The waiting crowd quieted as her pursuer climbed onto the rock behind her. A swirl of dust streamed from her hand and was instantly caught by the breeze. The cloud of what Trevor knew to be ash twirled into a vortex then dissipated into the wind. Trevor couldn't make out her features under her hat, but he expected Constance wore a smile and a few tears, and hummed a twenties tune to the Vancouver bum who had finally made it to Egypt.

The guard threw up his arm in front of his face while the ashes eddied around and past him. He dropped to his knees, chest heaving. Constance turned and knelt beside him. A handkerchief bloomed in her hand like a flower. She brushed off the man's clothing, and then assisted him to sitting. The two lingered on the block for ten minutes, Constance in motion the whole time as she talked. Her hands flapped in a manner already too familiar to Trevor. Finally, the two began their descent.

Trevor returned the binoculars to the American, who snatched them back with a look of contempt and strutted away, wife in tow. An hour later, Constance jumped the last step to the ground. Trevor studied her face and was relieved she appeared merely tired. Her feet crunched in the chunks of broken limestone and she stumbled. Her face was pale but she smiled at the silent waiting audience.

"She's an old lady," a woman murmured.

Trevor started toward Constance. He wanted to congratulate her, and then they could get on their way. But before he could reach her, two officers took her by the arms and led her off.

"Wait," Trevor called but they paid no attention to him. Damn it. He followed them across the grounds toward a low concrete metal-roofed hut, and then watched in disbelief as Constance and the men disappeared inside.

"Shit, shit, shit!" He threw the sunflower bag to the ground and kicked it three times, then picked it up from the dirt and headed to the waiting taxi.

EIGHT

❦ Trevor sprawled in the sand against the wall of what he had come to call the guard room. Windowless and roofed in corrugated tin, the cinder-block hut radiated heat like a pizza oven. Over the course of the past few hours, the sun had inched its way down from its zenith and a narrow ribbon of shade fell along the dusty wall, providing him with a measure of protection. On the other side of three sand-pitted steps, an armed sentry lounged against the same wall, ignoring Trevor's presence as long as he didn't try to enter the building. Trevor had christened the man "G.I. Joe" after the military figures Brent had smuggled home under the radar of their guardians. On Saturday afternoons, the two boys would transform the vacant lot next door to the house in Regina into a war zone with foxholes and bunkers for their static and inadequate army.

"You know, Joe," Trevor said. "I could use a cold beer. How about you? Ice cold, straight from the fridge. I'm partial to lager myself. They got lager over here in Egypt?"

Joe didn't answer. He slouched against the wall, the butt of his rifle resting in the dirt. Every so often, he would extract a package of Turkish cigarettes from his pocket. Over the past two hours a comfortable co-existence had evolved between the two men. Trevor found their one-sided conversation helped pass the time.

"Did you hear the one about the man taking the penguin to the zoo and his truck broke down?" Trevor doubted whether Joe had any idea about penguins, but what the hell, the guy also didn't speak English. "Well, another guy drove by and saw the man and the penguin. So—"

The door opened. Joe dropped his cigarette and jumped to attention. Trevor scrambled up from the dust. A tall, thin man with a moustache ran down the stairs, boots clicking on each step. When Trevor tried to follow him around the corner of the building, Joe grabbed his arm.

"What are you doing to her in there?" Trevor shouted. Minutes later, the man returned with a china teapot, a teacup and a ceramic dish of honey-coloured squares balanced on a tray. He clicked back up the steps and kicked at the door with the toe of his boot. When the door swung open, Trevor strained to see into the dark opening but before his eyes could adjust, it slammed once again in his face. Joe released his grip and Trevor flopped back into the dirt against the wall.

"Tea, Joe. She's drinking tea with your cronies. Talking their ears off with wild stories and I'm out in the hot sun, worried about . . . about torture."

Interrogation, that was the word he wanted. A jet trail arched across the cloudless sky above. "Bet that's my plane. Going to Nairobi. A simple business trip. If you ever run across an old woman with a pink wig, Joe, avoid her, avoid her like the plague."

In an hour the sun would drop below the horizon. Trevor contemplated his options if Constance had not appeared before sunset. Two wild dogs, similar to the coyotes he saw occasionally on his runs by the Bow River, but with larger ears, lurked at the edge of the desert beyond the pyramids. The scavengers eyed him warily with overt intelligence. Creepy. Maybe jackals. Like the dog-headed man from the museum. Looking for a free meal, a wayward corpse. He didn't relish dealing with them in the dark and he'd heard desert nights were cold, unlike the prairie in summer, where the mercury hit the top of the thermometer at high noon and only the insane attempted sleep in anything more than a sheet at night. He and Brent would lie awake in the stifling heat of the attic room at Aunt Gladys's, not daring to move, to touch, under the weight of the sultry air. Or they would climb out through the window, pull themselves onto the roof and scamper to the peak, knowing discovery by Uncle Pat meant a beating. The rooftops of Regina spread out before them, the glow of downtown in the distance. They yearned for a breeze, a breath of wind, to cool their sweat-drenched young bodies. On a clear night, the stars thick in a pulsating canopy over them, they rested on their backs, hands clasped behind their heads, and invented names for constellations, counted shooting stars, and fabricated stories about aliens. Trevor spoke in whispers, afraid of Uncle Pat's fury, Aunt Gladys's inevitable "What would your poor dead mother have thought?" Brent talked out loud, careless. He tempted fate. Dared Uncle Pat to find him, haul him from the roof and beat him. Brent always laughed when Uncle Pat hit him. The man's face grew red with the effort and the fury. In the end he threw down the stick and stalked from the room, roaring for his wife to deal with the boy. But they never got caught, at least not on the roof at night. Trevor wondered now if the stars shone a different colour in the desert and if he would see Orion.

The door opened again. A different guard clicked down the stairs, this one short and stocky, and loomed over Trevor. He gestured wildly at the canvas bag in the dirt beside Trevor's leg and jabbered in Arabic. When Trevor picked up the bag, the man yanked it from his hand, whirled, thundered back up the stairs and slammed the door behind him. The noise ricocheted across the deserted expanse. The tourists had roared off in their air-conditioned buses long ago, clouds of exhaust spewing into the searing desert air. Trevor's taxi was the one car left in the parking lot. He had promised the driver a twenty-dollar American bill to wait all night if necessary. The crook had argued for forty.

The door swung open a third time. One of the men stepped out and gestured for Trevor to come inside.

"About time," he muttered as he ran past Joe, up the steps

and through the open door. It took a moment for his eyes to adjust to the dim light in the room. The furnishings were as dismal as the desert landscape: a grey metal table, four metal chairs, and a file cabinet. Fine drifts of sand lined the edges of khaki-painted walls. A fan, too weak for relief, struggled to blow air around the cramped space. Three men hovered like ghosts in a corner. There was no sign of Constance. Her bag lay open on the table beside the teapot. One of the men, his olive-coloured face shiny with sweat, pointed to the floor, and Trevor stepped cautiously forward to look.

Constance was sprawled on her back, wig askew across one eye. She looked like a cadaver. Trevor's throat constricted unexpectedly; heat pressed at the back of his eyes. "You bastards," he muttered and crossed the floor to kneel at her side. His fingers hovered inches above her body as he searched his memory for Grade Ten gym class and the sessions on mouth-to-mouth resuscitation, an embarrassing joke at the time. Check pulse. Breathing. He rested his fingertips on the side of her throat but detected no pulse. His own heart thumped furiously in his chest. He picked up her hand and pressed two fingers against the inside of her bird-like wrist, relieved to feel a spidery beat. The shuffling Egyptian at Trevor's shoulder rubbed his forehead with his dark nervous fingers.

"What have you done to her?" Trevor demanded.

The man shrugged, pointed to the bag on the table and babbled in Arabic.

"Constance?" Trevor touched her face with a shaky hand, expecting the creased skin to be dry and rough, but it felt as tender as a newborn's.

"Constance?" Her name came to her from a distance, like a bird flying by so far away you could only see the wings flapping. Maybe it was one of her husbands come to collect her, but she couldn't make out which one. "Constance." Then she recognized the voice—Trevor—her new friend from the airport and she remembered she was in Egypt. Trembling fingers shifted her wig away from her face. She tried to open her eyes. There was something important she needed to tell him but she couldn't recall what it was.

"Constance. It's Trevor."

She forced one eye open a sliver; his face materialized as if through fog. He picked up her hand in his. "Are you okay?"

She nodded weakly, barely able to move her head, but the room, his face, were coming into sharper focus.

"Are you hurt?" he asked. "Did they hurt you?"

"No . . ." she groaned.

He spoke to someone else in the room as he supported her to sitting. "Bring water, tea, something for her to drink."

She turned her head. At the sight of the three men looking on in the background, she remembered what had happened. A feeling of panic flooded over her and she clutched at Trevor's shirt. "The boys, Trevor. My bag's empty. They've taken the boys."

NINE

❦ "I can't leave them," Constance argued, as the Egyptians escorted her and Trevor to their taxi. She had come all this way: her trip, her plans would be ruined. "I won't go," she insisted. But she was no match for large men with guns and Trevor was not helping.

"They didn't hurt you?" he asked for the third time. "You're sure they didn't hurt you."

When the taxi pulled out of the parking lot, she began to cry, thinking of the ashes of Martin and Donald, lost, discarded in a garbage dump or blowing off into the Sahara with nowhere to rest. The Egyptian desert had been a suitable end for Thomas, appropriate he would remain a traveller on the wind, but the other two had been so different, both men of habit who relished security.

"Where are we going?" Trevor asked the men in the front seat—the driver and one of the pyramid guards who had unexpectedly been ordered to accompany them. Neither man answered. The radio blared machine-gun Arabic punctuated with loud, shrill music.

She accepted the tissue Trevor handed her. He had been a gentleman since he picked her up off the floor of the hut. She appreciated it, but his unwillingness to confront the men about the boys infuriated her. "What about my husbands?" She blew her nose into the stiff grey paper.

"Don't worry." He drummed his fingers on the armrest. Out the window the dark road was illuminated by the urine glow of streetlights. "I wonder where what's-his-name—Abdul—is taking us?"

"His name's Haji," Constance snapped, irritated by Trevor's lack of respect. Haji and the other men had pressed her to explain about the pyramid. They threatened to charge her with breaking the rules, but she had resisted, relying instead on a string of stories about her children and Canada. She was proud of her evasive tactic, a modern-day Scheherazade. She'd come to like Haji over the course of the afternoon. He'd brought her tea and squares; they had played cards together. His English, which he had learned in school, was rather good.

"Haji, then," Trevor snapped back.

Constance fell into a brooding silence for the rest of the trip as she hunted through her mind for a solution to the situation. Perhaps the police would help her find the boys in the morning. There must be a Canadian embassy in Cairo. Twenty-five minutes later, when the taxi pulled up in front of the airport, her heart dropped.

"This looks promising." Trevor opened his door. Haji swivelled around in the front seat and held out his hand. "Passport? Ticket?" Constance and Trevor exchanged a glance, then reluctantly turned over their documents. Haji flipped through them and without a word led them from the taxi, into the terminal and up to the counter for East Africa Air where he conferred with the ticket agent.

"What is he doing?" Constance asked as she paced a circle around Trevor.

"Sending us to Nairobi if we're lucky."

"I can't leave the boys," she whined, feeling like an unruly child. She didn't care. There was no point in continuing without them.

She listened while Trevor sidled up to the desk and asked. "Are you putting us through to Nairobi?"

The agent nodded and stamped their tickets.

"Just how many flights a week to Kenya are there?" Trevor inquired.

"Three a day," the man replied and returned the documents to Haji.

Trevor sputtered. "The goddam liars."

Haji handed them their documents. "You leave Egypt now. Come again." He grinned and tossed Constance's suitcase onto the luggage conveyor. When he reached for Trevor's carry on, Trevor snatched it up.

"Me keep." Trevor gripped his bag to his chest.

Constance bristled at his reversion to pidgin English. Under other circumstances, she would have taught him something about manners and respect for other cultures, but now she had other things on her mind. She grasped Haji's arm. "You have my containers, one peanut but—"

"Let's go, Constance." Trevor pulled her away. "Our plane is boarding. Let's go before he changes his mind and throws us in jail."

Constance protested through security and across the transit hall where a crowd of tourists were arguing with Cairo Air officials, passports and tickets piled high on a desk. She heard Trevor mutter something about Egyptian-style tourism.

"What did you say?" Constance struggled to release her arm. "And let me go. I can't leave."

Trevor nodded his head toward Haji who hovered like a shadow behind them. "I don't think we have much choice." He guided her firmly by the arm through the double glass doors and across the tarmac to their plane. Haji followed them to the bottom of the steps and waited until the doors were closed and the plane in motion before heading back into the building. Constance could see him out her window, walking toward the terminal in the dark, a lone figure, her last connection with Egypt. The rock in her chest was as heavy as if she had suffered the death of another loved one. A feeling like no other.

Their seats were economy and the scotch cost Trevor five dollars each, but the money was worth it; Constance had stopped weeping, her forehead pressed against the window.

"May I borrow your whisk brush?" he asked. "My stuff's full of sand."

Without a word, she tossed the empty bag into his lap and resumed her sulking. He tucked the whisk into the pouch in front of him and pushed the satchel under the seat with his foot. He reached his carry-on down from the overhead bin and manoeuvred it into the narrow space between his stomach and the next seat. He unzipped the lid. Humming an aimless melody under his breath, he brushed bits of sand and dust from the two plastic bottles tucked in beside his change of underwear. Constance continued to stare out the window, but when Trevor raised the volume, he heard the anticipated rush of breath, a squeal and then her arms were around his neck.

"A thank you will suffice," he teased, ready for the praise, but instead, she slapped him on his arm with an open palm. "Ouch." He winced. "What was that for?"

"You should have told me right away, back at the pyramids," she scolded, lips thin and white with tension. "I worried myself sick about losing Donald and Martin. I thought they'd taken them. That I'd have to turn around and go home."

"Listen," Trevor protested. "I didn't want old Abdul and his cronies to find out about the ashes. Who knows, they might have suspected they were drugs and thrown you in jail. I took them out of the bag and left them in the taxi."

"Hmph." She flopped back against her seat, arms crossed.

Trevor bristled. His arm smarted. At least she could have thanked him. He had risked his own safety for hers, rescued her from a future in a filthy bug-ridden cell in some godforsaken prison, an uncertain fate. "You have no right to—"

A muffled sound from the next seat interrupted his objections. More tears. The passengers across the aisle glared at him. He held his tongue; the poor woman had been through a lot and he could understand her distress. Another strangled sound erupted from between her lips, then a third and she began to shake, gently and silently. He felt more helpless than when confronted with her still body on the guardhouse floor. He sighed, gathered a husband in each hand, faced the ceiling and its orderly arrangement of buttons, nozzles and lights, and said, I'm sorry, I—"

She snorted again, even louder this time. He stopped mid-sentence to look at her. Her hand was clasped over her mouth and tears ran down her face. A sound not unlike the bray of a donkey burst from between her fingers. To his astonishment he realized she was laughing.

"You should . . ." she gasped, barely able to speak through her laughter, "you should have seen that young man at the top of the pyramid. He was . . . wheezing. I thought he was going to fall over backwards when he saw he was chasing a granny." She dabbed at her face with a sodden napkin. "Poor boy. Did you know a tourist fell from the pyramid recently? And their president was assassinated not long ago. No wonder they have guns."

Trevor was beginning to appreciate why this woman had so many husbands. "But they didn't speak English. How did you—"

"Haji did. He was a mean poker player too. I lost ten dollars to him."

"You mean you played poker while I was outside in that inferno worrying that you were dead . . . or worse?"

"I'm sorry." She collected Donald and Martin from Trevor's hands and set them on her table. "Haji and his friends were armed. I had to keep that in mind." She squeezed his hand. "I knew you'd wait."

Trevor felt ashamed. He'd been fifteen minutes away in the taxi on the road to the airport before he'd ordered the driver to turn back to the pyramids and Constance. "You are in pretty good shape for a woman your—"

"Jazzercise. Every Tuesday and Thursday. And thank you, Trevor. For rescuing the boys . . . and me."

For a moment they sat without speaking, the hum of the jet engines filling the silence.

"I shouldn't have hit you," she said.

"No problem," Trevor raised a hand. "I deserved it."

"No," she insisted. "I'm sorry. I abhor physical violence."

The pilot's voice crackled over the intercom to announce they were over Sudan. The flight attendants would distribute snacks, magazines and drinks shortly.

"Donald hit me."

"Pardon me?"

"Donald. He hit me," Constance repeated. "Over new winter coats for the children. Can you imagine?"

The declaration left Trevor speechless.

"You're a neat person," she continued, confession already forgotten as she studied his open carry-on. He followed her gaze to the boxers and socks, folded not rolled, papers stacked, not a page out of line, alongside his navy toiletry bag, pens tucked into slots in the lid.

"I . . . I suppose. I like to have things in their place," Trevor muttered, confused by the change of topic. He wanted to back up a few sentences. To the part about Donald. The hitting. But he didn't know how to negotiate his way through the intimacy of a human conversation, the maze of vowels and consonants, nouns and adverbs, and the hidden minefield of unsaid words and implications. The sad weight of her words were as familiar to him as the back of his hand, for wasn't he the master of hidden grief. He bore the buried scars of Uncle Pat's willow stick, Aunt Gladys's biting words. The pummelling loss of his parents. This feeling belonged to him, not to this tiny buoyant woman. He wanted to whisk it from her and into his neatly ordered bag, to save her from the looming well of misery. But he didn't know how. "Yes . . . neat," he said lamely.

"People are all different, aren't they?" she said, cheerfully. "Donald was a neat freak. Never a thing out of place. He complained constantly about my clutter. Wish I'd had the nerve to tell him to clean the damn place himself." She chuckled. "And Thomas. Hopeless, everything a jumble, clothes and books all over the floor. He never slowed down long enough to clean. It's a wonder we never broke any bones walking through our apartment. Stop washing floors and come dancing, he'd say."

She shook her head. "Funny isn't it. I was the same woman, doing things the way I always did them, and to those two men, I was a different person. Martin and I did the housework together, which was much more fun. Remember that. I hope you and Angela will always do the housework together."

"Yeah, I'll try . . . to remember that," he murmured. Angela was as careless about her surroundings as her appearance. The night they met they had gone late at night to her basement suite in southwest Calgary. As they unbuttoned buttons, unzipped zippers, crushed against one another, she kicked clothes and papers out of the path of their passionate dance across the floor to the bed. She broke the embrace only to lean down bare breasted to toss more books, a pile of unfolded laundry and a plate with a half-eaten muffin to the floor before she pulled him onto the tangle of sheets and blankets. Since then, he made sure they always ended up at his place. He wasn't sure why he kept seeing her. Great sex? She took no interest in fashion, her hair perpetually mussed and falling into her face, fingernails cut short. He didn't think she owned an iron. One night, when he suggested she try a bit of make-up and a dress, she retorted that mascara and cleavage weren't going to win court cases, or men, and if it ever came to that, she'd quit both. To make matters worse, she tended toward strange dietary preferences. After their first sex, she disappeared into the kitchen and returned with a concoction of peanut butter and cheese on bread. When he had pretended to gag, he was surprised at the disappointment on her face.

"Hello . . . dream boy," Constance said in an attempt to attract Trevor's attention; the man seemed miles away. When he finally turned to her, he looked as if she had pulled a favourite toy away from him. "Dinner's here." She gestured at the flight attendant who stood in the aisle with their food. "I don't know about you, but I haven't had a thing but sweet tea, halvah and scotch since this morning."

Trevor passed her the tray. "Not to mention scaling a fifty storey pyramid," he added. "Whose next?"

"Up the pyramid?"

"No, which husband?"

"Donald," she answered. "He was second. But I don't know where. He was the difficult one."

"More difficult than Tom?"

"Much . . . more difficult." She held up two fingers to the attendant. "May we have more scotch, please." She didn't want to talk any more about Donald. She'd already said too much about his cruelty, his physical abuse. She'd never told a soul about the hitting until now, not even Iris. Maybe if he hadn't gone to the war it wouldn't have been so bad. "He didn't dance," she said. "How could I have been married for thirty-one years to a man who didn't dance?"

"But you did leave," Trevor said.

"Yes, I did." Those three short words sounded so simple. Yes, I did. But it had taken years. She squirreled away extra grocery money until the day Susan left home. Constance had packed her bags and walked out without a word to anyone, with enough cash to get to Victoria where Iris, an old high school friend, lived with her husband. She had been fifty-three years old with no skills or resources of her own. Iris helped her find an apartment and a job in a bookstore downtown. When the divorce papers arrived, she had celebrated with a half bottle of champagne, which she drank on a wooden bench overlooking the Strait of Juan de Fuca and the Olympic Mountains. The plaque mounted on the backrest of the bench read, *In memory of Joseph Smith, who loved the sea.*

Trevor raised his glass. "To your divorce."

She clinked her glass on his. "To my divorce." She took a sip. "Donald married Anna right away. I'm sure he had her on the side before I left."

"Bastard."

"I don't blame him. He sure didn't get any from me."

Trevor choked on his scotch; the amber liquid sloshed onto the crotch of his pants.

"You are much too serious, dear," Constance said with a smile and handed him a napkin.

TEN
Alberta, Winter, 1985

❦ Like a great mechanical raptor, the Boeing 747 circled above the snow-covered Alberta prairie, the city of Calgary pinned in place by its solitary tower and the cluster of downtown high-rises. Trevor rested his forehead against the oval window and searched the northwest shore of the Bow River for the three-storey walk-up in Sunnyside he called home. He'd been gone less than a week, but the unexpected events that marked this business trip as distinctly different had left him exhausted and off balance. He was even more thankful than usual to see the familiar grid of streets below and know that soon he'd be stretched out on his own bed after a well-deserved shower, thinking regular thoughts about normal life.

The past few days had been anything but normal, as if he'd fallen into a weird subterranean world, where people carried guns and the trickster came disguised as an exasperating old woman. His own fault though. He rubbed at the annoying smudge of lipstick on his shirt sleeve with a paper napkin and wondered how he could have broken his cardinal rule. *Don't talk to strangers.*

Except for the quilt of snow and the patchwork of roads that criss-crossed the monotonous land, the prairie from the air reminded Trevor of the Kenyan savannah. Twenty-eight hours ago he was leaning over the shoulder of Constance Ebenezer as they flew into the Nairobi airport at dawn, the woman barely able to contain her excitement as she pointed out the giraffes— he figured them for trees—and exclaimed over the red cast of the soil. She insisted she saw snow on the top of Mt. Kenya, its gently sloping flanks and three-peaked cone half obscured by cloud far in the distance. A big melon sun pulsed above the horizon, and the sky to the east flushed orange as they stood with their luggage in the open-air terminal. Trevor fumbled for a way to say goodbye then did something very unlike himself; he handed her a business card, his home address and number scribbled on the back. She kissed his cheek as a street vendor snapped a picture of them with Constance's camera. Before he could recover from the affectionate gesture, she headed for the local bus, an ancient rattle-trap diesel packed full of boxes and chickens. He swore he heard a goat bleat from inside. Black faces with dark eyes crowded the windows; people sat cross-legged on the roof, balanced on bumpers and hung out of the doorway. He had intercepted her and hailed a cab; then stood, hand raised uncertainly as her taxi roared into the African morning, clouds of exhaust spewing from the tailpipe.

Trevor cinched his seatbelt and gripped the armrests as the jet began its descent into the Calgary airport. The jagged silhouette of the Rocky Mountains stretched along the horizon to the west. The forlorn feeling that clung to him at their parting should have begun to fade into the muffling folds of time, but he couldn't help wondering where Constance might be now. He recalled her last words to him. As she slid into the taxi, he had ventured an awkward "take care." She leaned out the window, gloved fingers curled over the edge of the door, her hair a halo backlit by the morning sun, an undecipherable expression on her face. "No, Trevor Wallace. Take chances."

Trevor released his white-knuckled hold on the armrest as the plane taxied to a stop. Landings were better than takeoffs and at least this flight was depositing him home. He retrieved his luggage and filed down the aisle behind the other passengers into the terminal. As he picked a path through the stacks of luggage and waiting travellers in the baggage area, he kept his eyes down and alert. No mistakes this time. An instant of inattention had been his downfall. Literally.

The Canada Customs agent flipped open Trevor's passport,

stamped it and passed it back. "Welcome home, Mr. Wallace." Trevor almost kissed the man's hand. To be back in civilization was a wonderful thing. He counted himself lucky not to be languishing in an Egyptian jail.

Trevor couldn't wait to be outside in the clear Alberta air. The only thing that kept him from running the last few steps to the automatic exit doors was a lump in his left shoe. He stopped, removed the offending shoe and discovered a teaspoonful of sand, a souvenir from the Sahara. As he shook the fine pale blonde grains into a waste bin, he smiled, shrugged his shoulders and laughed.

The winter wind hit Trevor outside the terminal; the dry prairie cold seared his throat. He hailed a cab. The minus temperatures were almost a welcome relief from the desert heat, but he was underdressed and pulled up his collar, glad to slip into the warm taxi. On the drive into the city centre, his thoughts shifted from the events of the past few days to the tasks at hand. First sleep. Tomorrow grocery shopping, laundry, a call to Angela and a sales report for the trip. He was going to have to leave out a number of details. Andy would never believe the story. Maybe the whole thing was a twisted dream brought on by tainted food or jet lag. Back to dreamless nights and uneventful days. Thank God. And CE? A strange sweet woman. But he'd heard the last of her, he was sure of that. By the time the taxi pulled up in front of his apartment, the frozen Bow a comforting sight across the street, thoughts of Constance had dropped, like the sand from his shoe into the trash can, down the dark swirling void of his memory along with everyone else in his past.

Angela threaded her way through the crowded coffee shop toward him, her face glowing from the cold outside, blonde hair tucked up under a wool toque, battered briefcase under her arm. For some reason, he had been more anxious than usual to see her and had called her the same day he arrived home. But she'd been busy with a case, and it had taken over a week for them to arrange this short meeting for coffee.

"Hi." Angela dropped into the chair across from his. She appeared happy to see him. He had the strongest urge to lean across the table and kiss her, but to do so would have been out of the ordinary, at least their ordinary. He smiled back lamely and said, "How are you?"

"Way too busy." She shrugged off her coat. "My workload is out of control. But hey, good to see you." She ordered a coffee from the waitress and sat back. "How was your trip?"

"Wild."

"Wild? Doesn't sound like you." She pointed at the piece of carrot cake on the table in front of Trevor. "May I?" When he nodded she carved off a corner with a spoon and ate it, leaving a smear of cream cheese icing at the corner of her mouth.

Trevor wanted to lean over and brush it off, or lick it off for that matter, but instead he pointed at the corner of his own mouth. "Icing."

"Oh, thanks." Angela licked the white smudge with the tip of her tongue, an act which caused Trevor's blood to run a little faster. "So, are you going to tell me what wild means?"

"It wasn't really that wild. Just an unexpected layover in Cairo."

"Did you see anything interesting?"

"The pyramids," he answered; an image of Constance on the Great Pyramid suddenly flashed in his mind. It was first time he'd thought about her since he got home. "And the museum, but that's all."

"Doesn't sound too wild to me."

"I got buttoned-holed by an old woman who wouldn't leave me alone," he said. "And there was a god in the museum with a dog's head and man's body who weighs your heart when you die to see if you qualify for heaven."

"Weird." Angela sipped at her coffee. "I love all that stuff, you know, the rituals and the strange supernatural beings."

"Well, you wouldn't have loved Cairo," he said. "Dirty, armed soldiers everywhere, people trying to rip you off."

"I might," she said. "As if I'd ever get there with all the work I have." She looked at her watch. "Shit, I have a meeting in fifteen minutes. Sorry, I gotta go."

"Already?" Trevor felt strangely unsatisfied at the thought of her leaving. "Do you want to come over later?"

She was already pulling on her coat, the coffee only half gone. "I don't think I can manage it for a while." She pulled her hat on. Wispy strands protruded from the bottom edge like handfuls of straw. She slipped on a pair of bulky mittens that looked homemade. "I'll call you on the weekend, but don't count on anything." She tossed a bill on the table, then tilted her head, studying him. "You're looking great though, more . . . relaxed or something."

Trevor remained seated as she disappeared through the door. He wanted to get up and follow her, wanted them to spend the day together, but again it would break the rules, their understanding. He'd had other girlfriends, never longer than a few months, and he'd made the mistake every time of getting too serious too quickly. Each relationship ended in heartbreak for him, apparent relief for the woman. When he'd met Angela, she had seemed as anxious as he to keep things simple.

Trevor added some change to the money on the table and walked to his car. The streets were slippery with ice, the wind so cold he had to cover his ears with his hands. So far, their arrangement had worked well. He didn't want to screw things up. When he started the ignition, the car radio was playing a rerun of last week's hockey game; he turned up the volume and listened all the way home to his empty apartment.

Life for Trevor settled back into its comfortable pattern.

Work, exercise, *Hockey Night in Canada* and the occasional evening with Angela. When he didn't have trips scheduled, he manned the floor in the domestic salesroom, where he'd been for fifteen years since he moved from the Regina outlet. His promotion from janitor and go-boy to salesman and the transfer to Calgary had surprised everyone, not the least Trevor, who had taken a summer janitorial job with Forrester before high school graduation and still worked there seven years later. Occasionally asked to fill in on the showroom floor, salesmanship had proven to be his hidden talent. Before long he could rattle off the specifications for dozens of tractor models: engine capacity, transmission, drive train, horsepower, torque, tread size; all this despite the standing joke among the company mechanics that Trevor was incapable of even changing a spark plug. When the international sales position in Calgary had come open, the company manager had talked him into it. Trevor had doubts about the travel and its disruption to his routines, but the raise and the increased benefits were attractive. He found that, if he was efficient with his trip planning, he still spent most of his time at home.

At the beginning of March, Trevor returned home from an exhausting trip to South America to find a thick airmail envelope stuffed through the narrow slot of the steel mailbox in the lobby of his apartment building, along with a stack of bills and junk mail. He tossed the pile of mail onto his desk, showered and went to bed. He slept until noon, then went for a run along the river, so it wasn't until after dinner that he settled down with a glass of wine at his desk, the television tuned to the local news. The weekend stretched before him. Lots of hockey. The Stanley Cup playoffs were on: tonight Calgary played Edmonton. He might invite Angela for a drink if the game didn't go into overtime.

He shuffled through the stack of mail until he came to the envelope with its handwritten address and Nairobi postmark dated February fifteenth—over a month ago—no return address. He studied it, confused at the personal appearance of the letter. Clients never contacted him at home; he refused to give business associates his personal information. Work stayed at the office. That was the way he liked it. A personal letter addressed to him was more than rare; it was unheard of.

He slit open the envelope. Three items fell out onto the desk: two photographs and a folded sheet of delicate paper. A waft of perfume sent him back to the Nairobi airport, the premature heat of the rising sun, the noise of the people, the overcrowded buses, the scent of rose left on his cheek along with a smudge of lipstick before Constance climbed into the taxi, tear-stained handkerchief fluttering out the window as she set out for the Jacaranda Hotel and, he thought, out of his life. He couldn't help smiling. He hadn't expected to hear from her ever again.

He picked up the first photo. An African warrior hovered in mid-air, a foot off the ground, a band of red and orange print cloth wrapped around his muscular body from shoulder to hips. A lion's mane headdress flared from his head and swatches of red smudged his dark face. His legs were painted in an intricate pattern of lines and swirls; metal bells hung from his thighs and ankles. His lips were parted as if in song and a strand of red and yellow beads dangled from his neck across his sweat-shiny torso. His left arm lay rigid down his side, an object clasped between his right arm and his ribs. Trevor turned the photograph over. On the back, written in a chicken scratch he could barely decipher were the words, *Michael with Martin and Donald.* Trevor flipped the photo over again and examined the warrior with a magnifying glass. Two plastic bottles were nestled in the crook of the warrior's arm.

The second photograph was a shock. A tractor—one of

his tractors—a 1974 International Harvester model 1066, red and white, was parked at the side of a field. It had been sitting there for a long time; tall spikes of dry grass obscured the knobby tires. Constance was perched, legs crossed, on one of the wheel wells. She wore khaki pants and shirt, a pink scarf and her broad-brimmed hat. He recognized the sweet grandmotherly smile. Martin and Donald occupied the bucket seat.

Trevor unfolded the letter.

14 February, 1985
Sekera Village, Kenya

Dear Trevor:

Jambo Bwana (that means 'hello man' in Swahili).

I hope this letter doesn't take too long to get to Calgary. I wouldn't want you to think I forgot you. I'm anxious for you to see these pictures.

I don't know what I expected to find in Africa. Animals yes—and I've seen them all—elephant, giraffe, zebra, cape buffalo. Yesterday we watched a pride of thirty lions for an hour. Heaps of lionesses and their cubs. Magnificent and beautiful. But the hospitality of the people has overwhelmed me. The young man in the photograph is Michael; his Maasai name is Pakuo. You can see by the photo that he's a full-fledged warrior, but he also teaches English in the Continuing Education Program in the village. We met in a roadside café on the last day of my safari, and he invited me home with him for two weeks. I sleep in his boma with his family: his wife, Melissa, and their two children, Janey and Albert. I love the communal bed with the children cuddled against me, the bleating and shuffling of the calves and kids in the next room. I can't bring myself to drink cattle blood and milk for breakfast though, and I have developed a cough from the cooking fire.

I have a favour to ask you. Is this one of your tractors? It's broken. Nobody knows how to fix it. They've asked the government to send parts but it never happens. For the life of me I can't imagine why anyone would give tractors to the Maasai. They're nomads. Breaking the ground is against their beliefs. It's ridiculous they are being forced to settle in villages and farm. They hire Kikuyu to do their cultivating.

Would you please send a new starter to Michael at the above address? In fact, the next village has the same problem. Send two starters and a good assortment of parts. They also have no money for gas. Can you talk to one of your friends in Nairobi? We will be forever grateful.

One of the elders died last week. The relatives rubbed his body with lamb fat and made new sandals for him to speed him on his journey. They placed a cattle stick in his hands and laid him out in the open savannah, facing east toward the sunrise. Wild animals cleared away the body in the night. Simple, beautiful, proud and harsh—like their lives.

As tomorrow is my last day, Michael arranged a feast of goat in my honour with plenty of dancing and singing. Women aren't allowed to eat at the feast, but they made an exception for me. An eighty year old woman isn't much of a threat. Tomorrow I take the train to Mombasa and Malindi and the Indian Ocean. Might be a good spot for Donald.

Please say hello to Angela for me.

Love,

Your friend Constance

ELEVEN

〰 Trevor stared at the photograph. Send a random assortment of parts to a village out in the African bush? *What do I know about mechanics? I drive my car to a shop for an oil change; I'm a salesman.* He dropped the photos and the letter into a drawer. Constance was as eccentric as ever. He turned on the hockey game and settled onto the couch. His fingers smelled faintly of rose petals.

For the next couple of weeks, Trevor couldn't keep his mind off Constance and her letter. He found himself staring out his office window at the parking lot though he had a dozen reports to write up, trips to plan. In their regular Wednesday sales meeting, Andy asked him a question three times before Trevor noticed and fumbled for an answer. He couldn't put his finger on the problem. He wasn't worried about Constance. She'd had a lion-killing Maasai warrior guarding her for Christ's sake. Besides, why did he care?

His electric pencil sharpener brought the problem into focus. The sharpener quit, failed to sharpen. Instead of honing the pencil tip to a lethal, efficient point, the machine ground it away to a dull stub. He tried to fix the problem himself and ended up with a boxful of parts. The stock room assured him he could have a new one in a week, but instead, he carried a box of pencils into reception and sharpened them all, one after another. As he put the last pencil into the hole, the answer came to him. He hated broken things. Nothing stayed broken in his house for more than a day. He went out of his way to buy good quality furniture and reliable appliances from stores with efficient service departments. The thought of a tractor, one of his tractors, rusting on the plains of Africa, hyena piss on the tires, lion tooth punctures through the upholstered seat, was keeping him awake at night. He assured himself his anxiety had nothing to do with Constance and her favour.

He walked across the hall to talk to Andy who'd been with the company thirty-five years. Trevor tapped on the open door.

"Trevor," Andy said. His chair squeaked as he leaned back. He'd put on weight and the buttons of his shirt strained across his stomach. "What's up?" Andy never travelled any more. His hair had fallen out over the years Trevor had known him. He played golf on weekends and pictures of his grandchildren crowded the desk.

"Hi, Andy," Trevor sat down. "I have a suggestion. About follow-up."

"Follow-up?" Andy's bushy eyebrows crowded together in the middle of his forehead. "What do you mean?"

"Can we improve our follow-up on international sales?" Trevor wasn't sure what he was advocating. He never followed up on his overseas sales. "You know. Are customers satisfied? What do they do if they need parts?"

"That's up to the buyer," Andy said. "If they ask us for parts, we would send them but it's their responsibility. But that's not your worry. You sell 'em, Trev, I'm happy."

"We don't get many requests for parts do we? You'd think they'd break down once in a while."

"You'd have to talk to the parts department about that."

Trevor nodded slowly. "Well, thanks." He rose to leave, but Andy signalled for him to sit down again.

"Are you okay?" Andy crossed his arms. "You've had a lot of trips lately. I noticed you're . . . distracted."

"I'm fine," he answered.

"Well, think about taking a week or two off." Andy said. "We need our best salesman fit."

Trevor rode the elevator to the ground floor and skirted across the yard to the Parts and Service department. He didn't recognize the man at the counter, but the name *Sid* was embroidered on the man's green coveralls.

"Trevor, don't see you down here often." Sid said. "What can I do for you?"

Trevor was surprised Sid knew his name; he rarely came into the warehouse and didn't recall the man's face from staff gatherings. "Do we get many requests for parts on our foreign aid sales?" he asked.

"Rarely." Sid slipped his pencil behind his ear and looked at Trevor curiously.

"You'd think they'd break down once in a while."

"You'd think. But either the folks over there have other sources for parts or our tractors never break down."

"Doesn't that seem unlikely? We've sent hundreds of tractors over there the last few years."

Sid shrugged. "Maybe they're not very organized. You know those countries better than most." He leaned on the counter. "Anything else I can do for you?"

"One thing." Trevor reached into his pants pocket and drew out a slip of paper. "Listen, would you?" Sid tapped his pencil on a pad of paper. "Never mind." Trevor mumbled. "Thanks." He shoved the paper back into his pocket and walked away.

March 15, 1985
Malindi, Kenya

Dear Trevor:

There's a sign on the wall of the train from Nairobi to the coast that says, "No lunatic, whether accompanied by an attendant or not, will be allowed to ride on this train." By order The Lunatic Express. They let me on the train, dear. So you can rest assured I'm not a lunatic.

Here I am in the Indian Ocean. My guide, Rebecca, took the photo with an underwater camera. She agreed to bring the boys along in her net bag.

We made sure they were waterproof, airtight and buoyant. I couldn't bear to leave them on shore.

The water here is like a bathtub, unlike the ocean around Victoria where a person turns into an iceberg in five minutes. The reef fish come in bizarre shapes and amazing colours. If you float quietly beside the coral, you can hear the fish eat.

Last week I visited Lamu, a Muslim island south of the Sudan border, a romantic place with narrow winding streets and wonderful seafood. The Lamu craftsmen carve exquisite doors and furniture (see photograph enclosed). Miles and miles of white sand beaches and no people. I found a graveyard in a mango grove on the way to the beach. Muslims don't make much fuss about death, a plain cloth wrapping and prayers.

I've decided the Indian Ocean isn't the right place for Donald. Too much like heaven. You know, Trevor, when I think about my life with Donald, I feel embarrassed. That I let myself get into such a bad marriage. That I let my father and Donald push me into it. Women put up with things in those days. I'm glad young woman today are more assertive. I'm sure your friend Angela speaks her mind. And, I know you let her, bless your heart. I'm making up for it now though, aren't I?

Tomorrow I'm going back to Nairobi. My plane leaves for New Delhi on Wednesday.

A parrot fish followed me today. I named him Trevor, after you. I hope you don't mind. He made me feel safe.

Love,

Your friend Constance

Trevor and Angela rested side by side on their backs in the dark of Trevor's bedroom, slick with sweat and panting with the exertion of the past hour and a half. The bedding and both pillows had fallen haphazardly onto the floor beside the bed. Except for their breathing and the intermittent hum of the refrigerator, the apartment was silent. Outside, the sounds of Calgary at night were audible: the distant roar of the traffic on Blackfoot Trail, the occasional whistle of the CP train, the faint drawl of music from the cowboy bar just across the river.

"Peak performance," Angela teased.

"Mmmm, thanks." Trevor murmured. "You too."

Angela rolled over, slid off the bed and padded barefoot to the bathroom. Light spilled onto the bedroom carpet as she flicked on the switch. He turned onto his side and propped his head up on one elbow so he could watch her move. She had sexy legs. And a nice ass. Angela closed the bathroom door, the crack of light still visible along the bottom edge. The toilet flushed, and he could hear water splashing into the sink. His body felt relaxed and warm, as it did after a long run.

The bathroom door opened and she stepped out, the contours of her body silhouetted against the backlight. She crossed the room and picked her jeans up from the floor. Trevor liked the way she was wearing her hair longer and how it swung across her shoulders like a curtain and brushed the outside curve of her breasts. Beautiful in an unassuming way.

"What are you gawking at?" Angela said as she slid one leg into her jeans.

"You," Trevor said. "Where you going?"

"Home, like usual." She pulled her jeans over her hips and zipped up the fly.

Trevor patted the bed. "Come here."

"God, they must have slipped you a virility potion in Egypt." She shook her head and pulled on her sweatshirt.

"You haven't been the same since you got back from there. No, you got me beat. I can hardly walk."

"No, not that." Trevor said. "I mean, come over here and talk."

"Talk?"

"Yeah, talk."

Angela paused in the middle of rolling a green wool sock onto her foot. "Talk, at this time of night? I gotta get home and sleep. Besides, I don't feel like talking about work. Or hockey."

"We can talk about anything you like." Trevor smoothed the patch of sheet beside him. "Come on. It's Sunday tomorrow. One night?"

Angela dropped one of her running shoes. It fell to the carpet with a dull thump. She straightened. "Stay here? I thought we had an agreement."

"We made it, we can change it," Trevor replied.

"What?" She shook her head. "I have to be in court Monday at eight. I've got a lot of work to do." She picked up her shoe. "Are you all right?"

"Yeah, I'm okay."

"I mean, if there's anything wrong and you want to talk about it, I could stay for a while."

"No, nothing's wrong." Trevor sat up. "I wanted to ask you about your grandmother."

"My grandmother?" Angela wrinkled her forehead and her nose at the same time, a habit Trevor found newly endearing.

"Yeah, did you have one?" He sat up and tucked a pillow behind his back.

"Of course I had a grandmother," Angela answered with a note of exasperation in her voice. "Everybody has a grandmother."

"I didn't. I mean, not one I ever knew."

"Oh." She dropped her other shoe and eased down onto the end of the bed. "What's this all about?"

He shrugged. "I just asked about your grandmother."

"You . . . you've never asked me about my life before, except for work," she said. "Isn't that against the rules too?"

"Like I said, we made the rules. Did you see her much?"

"Much? Every day. My grandma lived with us. She took care of us while my parents worked the farm."

Trevor raised his eyebrows. "You grew up on a farm? So did I. Where?"

"You did?" She looked shocked, then caught herself. "Our farm is near Swede Lake, a couple of hours south of here. We grow wheat and alfalfa, a dozen beef cattle and chickens. And we plant a huge garden. I helped my grandmother with it when she was alive." Angela's mouth curved into a smile. "She was amazing."

Trevor leaned forward. "How? How was she amazing?"

"Well . . . she lived her whole life on that farm. She and my grandpa emigrated from Sweden and homesteaded the land. My mom and dad run it with my brother."

"But you didn't stay?"

"No, I went to law school."

"And your grandmother?"

"She died about eight years ago. A month after I got my law degree." Angela traced a pattern on the sheet with her fingertip. "You know, I think she waited for me to graduate. She insisted I go to university. About a week after convocation, she went to bed and didn't wake up."

"I . . . I'm sorry." Trevor ran his hand down her arm. She flinched and pulled away; a flush of colour spread across her cheeks.

"She . . . taught me everything about that farm. I spent the whole summer in the garden with her. We planted over an acre: peas, carrots, potatoes, corn, lettuce, beets, raspberries, strawberries." Angela giggled. "You wouldn't believe it, but I know how to can green beans."

"Yuck, green beans." He stuck out his tongue. "My mom used to can green be—" He stopped in mid-sentence. "Where did that come from?"

"Where did what come from?"

"That memory. I don't remember my mom, how would I remember she canned green beans?"

"Your grandma you mean."

"No, my mom. I don't remember any of them. My mom, my dad, my grandmother, my grandfather. All dead by the time I turned six."

"God . . . six." Angela let out a long, slow breath. "Who raised you?"

"My mother's sister and her husband. And I wouldn't call it raised. More like tolerated. But I had my brother, Brent." Trevor leaned back again and laced his hands behind his head. "I haven't seen him since . . . let's see . . . Aunt Gladys's funeral fifteen years ago."

"Where does he live?"

"I don't know. Last I heard he was driving trucks."

"So." Angela paused. "You're all alone."

"Yup." Trevor answered. "Except for Constance."

"Constance?"

"A friend. "

"I didn't think you had any friends."

"Of course I have friends."

"Name one."

"Well, there's Constance."

"Besides her."

"You."

"Is that what I am . . . a friend?"

He rolled forward onto his hands and knees and crawled across the bed toward her. "Stay?"

She shook her head but this time she didn't move away. They stared at one another. She searched his face, up and down, side to side, as if hunting for a sign in the way he held his mouth or whether the crow's feet at the corners of his eyes turned up or down. He slid closer. Her eyes widened as he tilted his head up and kissed her on the mouth, the first time he had ever kissed Angela without wanting sex. He drew in the scent of her skin, the texture of her lips, the warm breath from her nostrils on his cheek. He had the urge to give her something, but he didn't know what.

Without warning, Angela stood, and Trevor toppled over into the vacated spot on the mattress. She hopped on one foot as she pulled on a shoe. "I'm sorry, Trevor. I gotta go. This . . . this is too weird, you know. It goes against all our agreements."

Trevor slid off the bed to follow her into the living room, but she turned and raised her palm to him. "No, please, I can let myself out. I know I'm not ready for this. And I don't think you are either." She yanked her coat off the rack on the wall and slammed the door behind her.

Trevor turned the deadbolt and leaned his forehead against the door. Why did he kiss her like that? What was he thinking? He shouldn't have asked her to stay over. It went against all his principles. He walked across the darkened apartment to the living room window, and still naked, looked out over the Calgary nightscape. What did he want? To spend life alone? Hell, he didn't know where his one brother was in this world, his single friend a loopy old woman toting dead husbands around the world. Constance and her three husbands. Three. In one life. He hadn't had a single steady relationship. You couldn't call what he had with Angela a relationship. Their relating consisted of how good the sex was afterwards or who should have taken the slap shot. Angela was bang on. He didn't know how to talk about anything else but work and hockey. He wasn't ready. He wouldn't know what to do with a wife.

He turned back into the bedroom. And now Angela wouldn't want to see him any more. His body ached all over at the thought.

TWELVE

꙲ A neat stack of letters built up in Trevor's top desk drawer over the next few months. He'd come to look forward to these missives from around the world. The pages were always filled with interesting details about unusual people and exotic places, and he enjoyed her humorous references to her husbands. One Saturday afternoon at the end of May, feeling particularly lonely and out of sorts, he retrieved the letters from the drawer and reread them one by one. But instead of cheering him up, they left him with a feeling of guilt and regret. Constance always managed to say something that pulled at his heartstrings.

April 5, 1985
Benares, India

Dear Trevor:
Last Tuesday a temple beggar in Pune read my fortune. A mysterious man in my life will do me an enormous favour. I knew right away. You sent the parts to Michael, didn't you my friend? I have seen broken tractors here too. But I don't know who owns them or I would ask you to send more parts. You should talk to the people who make them and let them know they have a problem with breakage. Last week I saw one swarming with monkeys. An elephant would be much more useful in India; you don't have to buy them gas and their tires don't go flat.

I am visiting the spiritual city of Benares. Hindus believe cremation on the shores of the Ganges frees them from the cycle of reincarnation. The dying descend on the city by the thousands. Pilgrims come to bathe in the sacred waters. The steps of the riverbank are crowded with people: women in colourful saris wet to their waists, men in loincloths doing yoga or meditating, vendors selling drinks and food. Flaming pyres consume the dead and chanting relatives scatter ashes in the river. You can taste the strength of these people's faith in the air, even the poorest of the poor send their father, daughter, wife to a better place. No one seems to care that the river is polluted by human and animal remains and raw sewage. I was tempted to throw Donald in, but when I meditated on the question (I took lessons in Pune) I got a clear no. I would have coped better if I'd known about meditation when I was married to him. The Ganges must be off limits to hypocrites. Then my guide told me about sati, where the wife burns herself alive with her husband's body. I packed Donald back in my bag and told him to stay put. I'm sure the perfect place for him will come along.

I hope you're happy in Calgary. Tell Angela they have beautiful fabrics here. She strikes me as the type who likes to sew.

Take care,

Love

Your friend Constance

P.S. I snapped a photo of the boys and me riding an elephant for you, but it didn't turn out.

Why did Constance always have to mention Angela? He had no idea whether she could sew and now he'd probably never find out. He hadn't seen her since the fateful night he'd suggested she stay over. He picked up the latest letter that had arrived in the Friday mail. *Maybe elephants were more useful than tractors.*

May 12, 1985
Xi'an, Shaanxi Province, China

Dear Trevor:

Travel in China is difficult, crowded and confusing, the language barrier greater than I have encountered in other places. However, I found a young Chinese woman, Lin, at the University in Beijing who knows English and accompanies me to the permitted tourist attractions: the Forbidden City, the Great Wall, . . . all remarkable. Today I toured the mausoleum of Emperor Qin Shi Huangdi who ruled between 246 and 210 BC. Like the Egyptians, the Chinese rulers from that time believed in an afterlife. The mausoleum, which took seven hundred and twenty thousand workers and thirty-nine years to build, was Qin's way of ensuring a stylish hereafter. Thousands of life-sized clay warriors—the Terra Cotta Army—guard the tomb and hundreds of pits reportedly contain sacrificial remains of horses, servants and maybe even wives of the Emperor. The Emperor's tomb is still sealed and filled with treasure, reportedly booby-trapped.

I didn't think much of it. Another pompous man sacrifices people and resources to glorify his death. Emperor Donald would have me mouldering in a pit along with a few other wives and my children. It wasn't long ago in Canada a woman was the property of her husband. Thank goodness for the suffragettes. We've come a long way in a short time.

Li has invited me to her parents' home for dinner tomorrow night. Her father, an orthopaedic surgeon, loves to cook, and I've had it up to here with rice, so she's promised me some variety. She saved me from eating dog yesterday at a street kiosk.

I don't have you to keep me out of trouble, but at
least I have Li.

Next week I head south.

Love Constance

What on earth did dog taste like? He tucked the accompanying
photo of Constance on the Great Wall of China inside the
envelope and replaced it along with the others inside his
desk. Out of sight, out of mind. He couldn't stand clutter,
his apartment usually clear of the mess found in most homes:
the piles of magazines and newspapers, the dusty knickknacks,
articles of clothing shed on the back of a chair or the floor for
pure laziness, the kitchen drawer jammed shut with odds and
ends. He had chosen this apartment building for its orientation,
and for the name of the area, Sunnyside, where light flooded
through the windows for most of the day, revealing every dust
bunny, each window smear, all the crumbs under the table
missed while sweeping.

He wandered into the kitchen. The room was spotless,
the counters empty, the floor newly washed that morning and
shining. Not a single crumb or dust bunny. Clean, sterile, just
the way he liked it. His long face reflected back at him from the
polished side of the toaster. He slumped down onto a chair.
Where was his usual sense of satisfaction at the state of his
surroundings? Maybe a little colour would help. A painting
or two to distract him from his empty life. He drummed his
fingers on the empty table, then jumped up and strode back
to his desk. Pulling open the drawer, he fished through the
letters for all the photos. Back in the kitchen, he spread them
across the table in a fan. Constance on the Great Barrier
Reef; Constance with the Maasai; Constance surrounded by
mountains of cinnamon, red chillies and mangoes in a New
Dehli market. He grabbed his keys and drove down to the
mall where he bought a dozen unobtrusive fridge magnets from

the office supply store at the mall. As soon as he got home, he pinned the photos onto the door of the fridge in neat lines.

He stepped back and appraised his handiwork. He would need more magnets soon.

Another letter and a postcard of a stunned herd of sheep arrived the middle of June.

June 1, 1985
Rotarua, New Zealand

My dear Trevor:

I always wanted to wallow in a mud bath. The baths at Rotarua smell like sulphur but warm a body up and are rumoured to slow down aging. Is there hope for us if I can reverse myself forty years? (Aren't I shameful—tell Angela I'm joking). I didn't bring the boys into the mud. They're already too far gone.

You might wonder what it was like having three spouses, not ever having had a wife yourself. I'm not suggesting you're a man of a certain persuasion, but if you were, I would still like you. I don't care about those things. I admire a kind heart and you have one of the kindest I've encountered. I'll never forget how you rescued me from the Egyptians.

In my youth, I thought when a relationship ended, whether due to death or divorce or plain boredom, the person went away and you forgot about them. I was wrong. When each of my husbands left, they took a Martin, or Donald or Thomas-shaped chunk out of me. A hole in my soul, the missing chunks orbiting around me like moons around a planet. Every once in a while one circles into my consciousness and I remember that person.

Good memories, bad memories. I don't will them, they . . . happen. I might be walking along the street in a strange city and Thomas waltzes into my head. Or I'm on my knees working in the garden and suddenly there is Martin in the next row forking the potatoes. I'm a woman full of holes with three moons orbiting. I can never get away. But it's also precious; even Donald gave me a gift. His cruelty taught me to value myself.

The best is to find a person who never leaves, who allows you wholeness, but that's impossible. Everybody dies sometime. I hoped this trip, the scattering of my three husbands in faraway places, would rid me of the orbiting pieces. Let me find myself in all the planetary debris. So far it hasn't worked.

I hope you and Angela will be whole together.

Love Constance

Trevor stuck the new photo to the fridge: Constance peering at him from a mask of mud. *Holes in the soul.* The notion might explain the uncomfortable sensation he had felt for the last few weeks. An Angela-shaped hole. It startled him. He prided himself on his control with women. Don't get involved. Danger. Keep your distance. But she hadn't returned his calls. No lunches in downtown bistros. No sex. He imagined the wind flowing through that shapely cookie-cutter gap in his soul. Did he have holes for his mother and father, another for Brent? A veritable Swiss cheese of missing persons.

He stretched out on the couch, the phone in his lap. She might not be home. She wouldn't want to talk to him anyway. Why would she? She made it clear—they had made it clear—their relationship was physical. Neither wanted to get involved at a deeper level. He had overstepped the line.

He lifted the handset.

He would tell her he had made a mistake in a fit of insanity, a brain parasite picked up in Africa. He would behave himself, he vowed, and dialled her number.

"Hello, Angela? It's Trevor."

"Trevor." Her voice was cautious. "Hi."

"I'm wondering. How about breakfast this Saturday?"

Breakfast was simple, non-committal.

"This weekend? I . . . I can't."

The rejection, swift, cruel. Forever an Angela-shaped hole in his solar plexus.

"How about during the week?"

Silence.

"I'm sorry. My brother's sick. I'm home at the farm every weekend to help. I'm getting behind at work. I can't."

"Oh."

He waited for the suggestion he call in a week. The offer to phone him when she had time. It didn't come.

"Well, give me a call when you have time," he said lamely.

"Sure. Is that all?"

"Yeah, that's all."

"Okay."

"Bye."

He hung up the phone—a complete shut-out.

Trevor ploughed through the puddles on the muddy trail through Fish Creek Park. Normally he would jump the puddles, but today he allowed the black water to spatter a line up the back of his thighs. He was getting to the thirty-five minute mark in his run, when the endorphins kicked in and flooded his body with a rush. He ran for the rush, the exhilaration, and the tight flat neat appearance running produced. He didn't care much for the swaying oblivion brought on by excess alcohol. Brent had tempted him with marijuana in high school, but he'd resisted. He preferred this natural high. You stopped running, it went away. It didn't wreck your liver, wipe out your memory. Running put a positive spin on life. He needed it today, a run to clear his mind, raise his spirits. It wasn't about Angela. He had changed the rules without her agreement. He could justify her reaction, but there was more. A restless animal prowled his body; a stalking tiger, a lion, crept up on him when he wasn't paying attention, its long sinewy body slinking through the grass, muscles primed to pounce. He was too young for a mid-life crisis. He didn't feel stressed at work. He would see his doctor. How would he explain it? Hey Doc. My cells are realigning. It started with a trip to Egypt with an old lady and her dead husbands. What's the diagnosis? An evil spell?

A mule deer, startled by his approach, bounded across the trail in front of him, its tail flashing white. He had seen coyotes here too, on the prowl, like the animal that had taken up residence in his body, and had heard that cougars roamed into the city along the creek, though he'd never encountered one. The new aspen leaves above his head trembled silver and green in the breeze, and wild rose grew thick along the edge of the trail. Trevor sucked in the sweet spring scent with every breath. Then he felt it, the sudden flood of energy through his veins, the perception he could run forever along this muddy trail, leaving behind the churning uncertainty in his gut. He had to run more. That was all.

When he arrived home, he found a phone message from Angela. *Call me.* The sound of her voice on the message made his heart pound faster. Had she changed her mind?

After showering, he wrapped a towel around his waist and anxiously dialled her number for the second time in a few hours.

"Angela? It's Trevor."

"Hi."

Silence followed, as if she were waiting for him to speak.

"You left a message to call?"

Had he misunderstand the simple words? *Call me.*

"I . . ." She cleared her throat.

He'd never heard her sound so nervous before.

"Listen. Would you like to come up to the farm this weekend? We're baling an early cut of hay and could use help. I . . . you said you used to live on a farm. I thought . . ."

"Sure, I'd love to."

"You would? Great. Can I pick you up after work on Friday? About five-thirty?"

"Okay."

"Bring old clothes."

Trevor dropped the phone onto its cradle and ripped the towel from around his waist. He swung it over his head and gave a jubilant whoop, then danced his personal version of the rumba down the hallway to the bedroom.

THIRTEEN

ᵂ Willow Bunch, Gravelbourg, Carrot River, Assiniboia. The names appeared one by one in Trevor's head like the power poles that flashed by the car window. The names didn't match the place signs along the grid of gravel roads though, but belonged in another province, an earlier time. Moose Jaw, Yellow Grass, Limerick . . .

Saskatchewan. Young Trevor waited at the edge of the prairie. He was four, maybe five. He strained to see to the end of the grassland where the world stopped, where land ran smack into sky. He wanted to walk to the horizon, to find out if it rose like a wall, or if you fell right off the edge into outer space. But he was afraid to take a step, for fear he might crush the flowers. The petals of a prairie crocus poked through a remnant of snow beside the rust-coloured toe of his rubber boots. A million crocuses coloured the ground purple in every direction, each pushing up through its own scrap of snow. The air smelled like dirt—wet and earthy with the promise of spring—and tickled his nose. It smelled like prairie dog too, but all he could see of the shy tan rodents were the mounded edges of their dens, perforations in the earth between the flowers. The boy wondered if prairie dogs loved crocuses too.

"Almost there." Angela's voice pulled him back inside the car, away from the name Assiniboia, away from the sea of crocuses. Outside, the late spring prairie stretched green, not purple before them. Fields of fresh-cut alfalfa dried in tumbled swaths behind barbed wire fences. Other fields were dotted with hay bales: golden blocks like giant shredded wheat cereal, or rolls of oversized cinnamon buns that cast long shadows across the striations left by the mower. The flat countryside radiated out to the horizon in every direction, divided into a grid of farmland by endless gravel roads. Stones kicked up against the underside of the car and a trail of dust followed them across the land.

"Did you say something?" he asked.

"We're near the farm." Angela glanced over at him. She hadn't said much since they left the Calgary city limits. "Were you asleep?"

"Daydreaming." He stretched his arms over his head and yawned. The radio played country music on low. They hadn't kissed when she picked him up, but she had grinned when he tossed his bag into the trunk of the car.

"Staying a month?" She had nodded toward his bulging hockey duffel.

Every few miles they passed a farmhouse with a line of trees along the drive, a red and white barn, a few outbuildings, an expanse of lawn, machinery parked in the yard. Most of the operations were well kept, the lawn cut, road graded and gravelled, flowerbeds around the house. Occasionally, they passed a windblown unkempt farm where the lawn was overgrown and dotted with thistle and dandelion, and the broken eavestroughs swung from the roof. The sight of the farmhouses unsettled Trevor with an odd sensation of familiarity.

Angela turned left without signalling, down a gravelled poplar-lined drive that circled around in front of a two-storey clapboard house. A black and white dog ran barking from beside the front porch and danced back and forth in front of the car, nipping at the tires.

As they stepped from the car, the dog jumped up on Angela's leg; she knelt and ruffed up the hair on both sides of his neck while he licked her face. She kissed the dog's nose and nudged him toward Trevor. "Meet Caesar A." The dog wound a figure eight between Trevor's legs and then sat down, long pink wet tongue hanging from his mouth as he panted. "He's a coy-dog, half coyote," Angela offered, then turned as the screen door squealed open and a tall woman, grey hair tied back in a loose bun, stepped onto the porch. She shaded her face from the evening sun with her hand.

"Angie," she called. "Didn't expect you till dark. Who's that you got with you?"

Trevor swallowed at the sight of the woman. In his enthusiasm to be with Angela, he hadn't considered that other people lived on the farm. People he would have to converse with. Did he think the farm was run by cows or chickens? That they'd have a cozy little farmhouse to themselves? He hadn't visited a private home since Aunt Gladys's funeral and the hostess had been dead, Uncle Pat long gone to lung cancer. Trevor and Brent had shared the twin beds in their old attic room to avoid the silent bedroom on the main floor and the ghosts of their aunt and uncle sighing through the hallways with the wind at night. The old house had still smelled like Uncle Pat's cigarettes. The brothers gathered up all Aunt Gladys's crocheted doilies and burned them, along with the willow stick they'd found in the corner of the porch, in the barrel at the back of the house. But this woman was very much alive and examined him from head to toe with eyes that wouldn't miss a naked flea.

Angela climbed the wooden steps to the porch and kissed the woman. "Mama," she said. "I brought muscles for the weekend. This is my friend Trevor. Trevor, my mother, Helen."

The woman thrust out a large rough palm. "Come in, Trevor. Welcome. Angie doesn't bring friends home much any more. Are you a lawyer too? Angie, you sure he can handle a bale of hay?" Her voice had the sing-song rhythm of a Scandinavian.

"Now don't give him a hard time," Angela said. "He's

barely in the door yet. We'll whip him into shape. Where's Dad and Bo?"

"Down in the south field checking the hay. They hope to bale by Monday. The rest of the fields are ready," Helen answered and opened the screen door.

"How is he?" Angela's voice dropped an octave.

"Best a person could expect I s'pose." Helen shooed them through the door.

As Trevor stepped into the kitchen, the sense of déjà vu nearly bowled him over. The milk separator in the corner, the green and black checkerboard linoleum, the cast iron cookstove, the old crank phone on the wall, the flowers on the windowsill. If he opened the cupboard door beside the sink, he knew he'd find cereal and a pot of wildflower honey.

"Axel, we got company," Helen sang out as she strode across the room to the oven, her movement almost manly as she pulled it open. The sizzle and aroma of roast meat wafted into the room. "Get a shirt on."

The smell of the meat, of the cookies on the cooling rack on the counter, the aroma of perked coffee in an aluminum pot on the stove mingled in Trevor's memory like old friends. A lean white-haired man in suspenders and a cotton undershirt was reading a newspaper in an upholstered rocking chair beside the cookstove. He rose, stooping slightly; his paper and glasses dangled from his hand.

"Dad, meet Trevor." Angela gave her father a quick hug. "Don't worry about the shirt. Trevor, my dad Axel."

Axel towered over Trevor, his grip like a vice, but his voice was soft and almost shy, rising and falling in the same musical way as Helen's. "Welcome to our home, son."

"Nice to meet you . . . sir." Trevor stammered. Uncle Pat had always insisted they call him sir.

"Only sir on this farm's the rooster," Helen quipped as she set a stack of plates on the table. "Angela, take Trevor up and get him settled," she said. "You can have Bjorne's old room. Do you drink coffee? Course you do. You don't look like one of those health food nuts. Supper in an hour. Roast beef. Homegrown."

Angela and Trevor hauled their bags up the steep narrow staircase. The warped wooden boards creaked with age. Trevor had to duck for the low ceiling and he wondered if Axel ever climbed to the second floor. Angela indicated the doorway on the left.

"That one's yours," she said and grinned sideways at him. "My folks are pretty old-fashioned. Throw your stuff in there, and I'll give you the grand tour."

Trevor stepped into the room. The attic ceiling, which sloped away to a gable window, reminded him of the room he had shared with Brent in Regina. He tossed his bag onto the single bed and reached across the wooden desk to lift the casement window. The fresh scent of mown grass and the chirp of crickets displaced the warm stale air. A row of hockey trophies lined a shelf above the bed and he picked one up to read the inscription. Bjorne Steffansson, Most Valuable Player Brooks Junior League, 1964.

"Bo was a great hockey player." Angela leaned against the door frame. "I'll get sheets after supper."

He wanted to ask her why she brought him here. The doorway framed her body. The faded print on the wallpaper matched the colour of her ponytail, and wisps of errant hair curled away from her face. In T-shirt and shorts she looked more like a teenager than a thirty-two-year-old lawyer. He wanted to kiss her. To ask her if he could. Instead he said, "Where will Bjorne sleep?"

"In the new house past the barn," she laughed. "He lives there with his wife and their three kids."

"What's wrong with him?" Trevor asked, fighting the urge to wrap his arms around her.

"He had a heart attack a couple of months ago, and he's

supposed to go in for bypass surgery when he's strong enough."
She turned. "Come on. I want to show you around before dark.
We won't have time to sightsee tomorrow."

The sun burned a hole in the flat blue page of sky above the
western horizon as they walked toward the barn, their feet
crunching in the gravel. Caesar A. followed, his paws inches
behind Angela's heels. A tabby kitten licked a stockinged
paw at the door of the barn as they passed. Around the corner
of the barn, a paved road split off from the main drive to a
modern split-level bungalow with a double car garage and a
basketball hoop in the driveway.

"Bjorne's house?" Trevor guessed.

Angela nodded. "There's three houses on this farm. My
grandparents homesteaded the land and built the log cabin
down by the coulee. My parents built their house when they
married, and we all lived there until grandma and grandpa
died. Bjorne and Nancy moved into the new house before Jake
was born."

"And Angela, where's her house?" Trevor ventured.

She put her hands in her back pockets and looked away. "A
basement suite in Calgary?"

A maroon half-ton pickup rounded the corner of the barn
and pulled up short behind them. A man stepped from the
driver's door, his blue eyes a blaze of light in a face weathered
by years of sun and wind. Another Viking, taller and leaner
than Axel. Trevor wondered how Angela got her light frame
in this clan of giants. And her dark eyes. The man wiped his
hands on his grease-stained jeans, tipped back a dirty red ball
cap, flashed a grin full of white teeth, and strode over.

"Angie," he yelled as he lifted her up and swung her
around.

"Careful," she yelled back at him, laughing, her hands
pressed against his shoulders. "Bo, put me down. You're going
to do it to yourself again."

"Oh get out, Ang," he protested. "I'm fine." He held out a work-roughened hand to Trevor. " Hi. I have to compensate for my sister's rudeness and introduce myself. Bjorne Steffansson."

"Trevor Wallace. Good to meet you." Bjorne's handshake was even firmer than his father's.

Bjorne raised his eyebrows. "Long time since you brought a man home, Ang. Are you two . . . ?"

"Bo," she scolded. "Trevor's a friend. He used to live on a farm. I asked him to come out and help hay, that's all."

"Okay, okay . . . friends." He grinned. "Ma asked me to send you two back for supper. By the way, a cayoot got one of her chickens last night, but don't tell her. I'll see you in the morning. About six."

He kissed Angela on the forehead, folded his body back into the pickup and tipped his cap as he drove past them to his house. When they turned back toward the old farmhouse, dusk had fallen over the yard and frogs sang from a distant dugout.

FOURTEEN

❦ Trevor hiked an endless plain. With each step, spear grass bent under his feet and the smell of sage lifted on the warm wind. In the distance a herd of bison grazed. Daisies waved their heads in the breeze and carpets of flax and beard-tongue rolled into the distance with the land. He walked the upward slope of a round-topped hill. At the rise, a cairn of stones, red with iron, directed his gaze into the cobalt canopy of sky where cotton ball clouds circled over his head. On the far side of the hill, an elephant laboured toward him; heavy feet cast billows of dust into the air. A woman sat astride the animal's back. Constance. She waved and called to him. The elephant encircled Trevor's waist with his trunk, and swung him around and into place behind Constance. Trevor looked down. He was not an elephant's height above the ground, but that of a hundred elephants, the prairie spreading below them like a map, the contours the shape of a woman's naked body, the earth below the mammoth's enormous feet the smooth skin of her torso, the hill a mounded breast. As Constance faced him she became his mother, and then not his mother but Angela, whose colourless hair billowed out behind her into a charcoal sky.

"Trevor." Angela leaned over him, her hand on his arm. The elephant vanished, and Trevor found himself curled up in an unfamiliar bed, the thin light of dawn filling the room.

"Time to get up, sleepyhead," she whispered. "Breakfast is on the table."

The smell of bacon and coffee, the clink of dishes, a radio voice and the scrape of a chair leg drifted up the stairs to his room. He shook his head to rid it of the remnants of the dream. Another damn dream. Three, four? He'd lost count.

"You'd think I'd hauled you out of a well. We don't want to keep Bo waiting," Angela said twisting her hair into a braid as she walked out the door. "See you downstairs. You'll need a good breakfast."

Trevor wedged his gloved fingers under the parallel strands of twine and heaved the eighty-pound square bale off the prongs of the forklift. He balanced it across his knee the way Angela had shown him, then hoisted it onto the stack in the back of the truck. Beside him, Bjorne's oldest son Luke, a beefy blonde teenager with a round head and freckled face, waited for the second bale. Angela drove the forklift, her face red from the heat under a denim ball cap, the sleeves of her shirt rolled up to her elbows. After Trevor and Luke lifted the bales from the forks, she spun the steering wheel and manoeuvred around the truck to the next bale in the row. Halfway up the field, Bjorne steered the baler along the rows of dried alfalfa. The machine scooped up the swaths then shaped, cut, bound and deposited the neat brick out the back. Axel drove the truck, jumping out every few minutes to direct the construction of the stacks. "Can't lose a load on the road," he said.

Trevor pushed back his borrowed ball cap and wiped his forehead with his sleeve. The day had begun cool at six, but now, at mid-day, the sun pounded down on their heads. His shoulders ached and, in spite of the gloves thrown to him by Bjorne that morning, blisters swelled at each finger joint. Breakfast sat like a weight in his stomach; Helen had pressed bacon and eggs, toast, jam and coffee on him followed by a stack of pancakes and syrup that Hercules would have appreciated. He passed up the sandwiches at morning tea, delivered by Bjorne's wife Nancy on a motorbike, but he knew lunch would arrive the same way in a few minutes and, though not hungry, he'd be grateful for the rest.

Bjorne, Angela's father, Nancy, even Luke scrutinized his every move, sized him up, judged him. The way he hefted the bales, whether he got their jokes, the fact he wore sneakers and not boots. Data into their inventory. He wasn't sure what it was all about. Hadn't Angela made it clear he was a friend? A friend. As she manipulated the fork-lift, he couldn't help but feel aroused by how she looked in her jeans and a denim shirt, three buttons undone. He shook out his shirttails to hide his crotch. He didn't dare complain of fatigue and blessed the set of weights in his closet at home and his ten-kilometre runs. They wanted to see how a city guy could work, he'd show them. He heaved the next bale up with all his might. It toppled off the other side of the truck, and onto to the ground with a thud.

"Hey, strongman. Careful." Angela sprang lightly from the forklift and heaved the eighty-pounder up to him with practised technique. He had never imagined the sight of strength in a woman could turn him on.

"And this is the Saskatoon berry," Helen said, serving Trevor his third piece of pie and ice cream. She ignored his protests. She had made three pies and insisted he try them all. Trevor struggled to stay awake after the day in the field. And Helen's supper: fried chicken, potatoes, gravy, green beans, green salad, coleslaw, bread and butter pickles, buns and pie. Why weren't these people enormous? The supper conversation had solved that mystery for him. Sheer hard work.

"My parents sailed from Sweden to New York." Helen served him the information along with a dollop of mashed potatoes and ladle of gravy. "Couldn't rub two pennies together between them. They walked to Minnesota and from there up to Alberta to the coulee east of here."

After the meal, Angela cleared the dishes and ran water into the sink. Trevor rose to help, dishes having been his job in Regina since he was five.

"Stay put," Helen insisted as she walked into the kitchen from the living room, arms laden with photo albums. Axel and Bjorne grunted, excused themselves and headed out to the west porch, "for the sunset," they claimed. Nancy shooed the children outside, then discretely followed.

"We got pictures back to 1930." Helen dropped the albums on the table in front of Trevor. She opened the first one and pointed to a black and white photo. "My parents." The man, tall and broad-shouldered like Axel, wore a mane of pale hair and looked into the lens like a startled deer, his arm around the slight shoulders of a determined-looking woman who wore her hair loose and smiled broadly up at her husband. An older Angela. Trevor now understood where she got her looks and her dark eyes.

Trevor flipped slowly through the worn pages as Helen commented on each photo.

"That's Matthew." She pointed to a picture of a thin, shy teenager on a tractor.

"Matthew?" Trevor asked.

"Our middle boy," she said. "He teaches at an agricultural school in Ontario. Doesn't come home much; but Axel and I visited last year. He's got two girls."

Trevor looked over at Angela, who appeared lost in thought, a dishtowel around her neck, forearms fuzzy with dish suds. She'd never mentioned there was a second brother, but then he'd never asked her about her siblings.

Trevor lingered over the photos of Angela: the tow-headed baby in her father's arm on a plank swing, the toddler with a mouth full of garden dirt, a four-year-old in a haymow with a fat puppy. The school class photo with her hair, almost white, in a fly-away pixie cut, one kneesock around her ankle. As a preteen, she'd been an earnest tomboy in jeans and pigtails, always an animal—dog, chicken, pony, puppy—in tow. He stopped at a photo of Angela grooming a calf. She was wearing her lawyer look, the eyes that could see through skin and bone.

"You haven't changed much," he teased. She stepped back from the sink and snapped his leg with the end of the towel.

"Hey," he laughed, then turned another page. Angela wrapped around a short man in cowboy boots. "Who's this guy?"

Angela leaned over for a look. "Never mind," she said, "That's enough of that." She gathered the albums up in her arms and disappeared into the living room.

"I missed your graduation photos," he called after her.

"You'll find those on the china cabinet," Helen assured him. "And her university one too." Helen pushed back her chair. "I guess I better get the bread on."

"Why'd she take them away?"

"I suppose she doesn't want to introduce you to her other men." Helen poured a measure of wheat kernels into an electric grinder.

"What do you mean?"

"Don't worry." She flicked a switch and yelled over the noise. "You're not missing much."

Trevor wandered over to the screen door. His legs were stiff and his arm muscles ached. Outside, he could hear Bjorne and his father talking on the porch. The two men smoked side by side on a wooden bench, discussing the merits of round bales over square. A guitar leaned against the wall next to Bjorne.

"We need to switch to round bales soon, Dad," Bjorne argued. "Everybody's doing it. We won't have a market soon."

"Our equipment's still fine," Axel replied. "The cattle don't care if the bale's round or square."

When the door slammed, both men pulled the cigarettes from their mouths, then chuckled and replaced them when they saw Trevor.

"We thought you were Ma," Bjorne said.

The screen door squealed again, and Helen appeared behind Trevor, a bucket of kitchen scraps in hand. "Trevor's smart. He doesn't smoke," she chided her son and husband. "He knows what's good for him. Was that cayoot after my chickens last night?"

"Don't worry Ma. I boarded up the holes," Bjorne answered. "And you know I've cut down smoking. Besides, Dr. Adams will fix me up good as new. And you give Trevor one more piece of food and he's useless to us tomorrow."

Helen looked down at the bucket confused. "These are for my hens," she said, then noticed the grin on her son's face. "If you weren't so big I'd spank you." She cuffed him affectionately on the top of the head and strode off toward the barn, grumbling to herself.

"Bye, Ma," Bjorne called after her, then stubbed out his cigarette and picked up the guitar. He turned to Trevor. "Ang mentioned you grew up on a farm. Where 'bouts?"

"Southern Saskatchewan. Near Moose Jaw." It was safer to stay vague. "Do you play much?"

"Much as I can. Which means not much with the farm and the family." Bjorne strummed a few minor chords.

"He had his own band in high school," Axel interjected.

"That was a long time ago," Bjorne answered. "So tell us. How'd you meet Angie? Law school?"

Trevor didn't want to tell them the truth. That they met in a bar. That they picked each other up at a smoky Calgary tavern. That they went home to her apartment and had sex that night. And wrote the rules. Nothing serious. Casual sex, drinks once in a while. No emotional stuff. He couldn't tell them that. This wholesome family wouldn't welcome this news about their youngest child and sister.

"No, we met through a mutual friend," he lied.

"Oh yeah," Bjorne finger-picked a half-dozen random notes. "You not a lawyer? What do you do?"

"I sell farm equipment."

"Farm equipment?" The two men look at each other. "Whee-hah, you're not one of those high priced namby pamby lawyer types Angie hangs out with?" Bjorne crowed, and put down the guitar. "Farm equipment we can relate to."

"What company do you work for, son?" Axel asked.

"Forrester."

Axel nodded approvingly. "Good company."

"What do you got new this year in the way of tractors?" Bjorne said.

"Are you in the market for one?" Trevor replied, happy to finally have some positive attention from the two men. "I noticed the tractor you have in the barn is pretty old. It looked like about a 1968 Case."

"1965. Dad keeps them going until they disintegrate," Bjorne joked. "I was driving it out in the north field last week and parts kept falling off behind."

"Don't go telling stories. No use wasting hard-earned money," Axel argued. "It might be old but it does the job."

"What you got for balers?" Bjorne winked at his father. "Round balers."

Axel grumbled under his breath.

"The John Deere 530 just came out." Trevor felt himself click into sales mode, his spiel smooth and confident. "Single twine, with an optional bale cutter."

"What kind of clutch?"

"Slip clutch. 1000."

The two men peppered Trevor with questions. They

discussed tractor power, combine capacity and cultivator efficiency, and made suggestions for improvements until the sun dropped below the horizon in a blaze of colour. Angela rescued him with a reminder that work started at dawn Sunday. Bjorne playfully cuffed him on the shoulder. "You take care of my little sister."

Trevor tried not to grimace at the assault on his overworked muscles and managed a smile. Bjorne winked.

Trevor felt like he'd passed a test.

Trevor pushed the casement window in his bedroom wider to encourage a wisp of breeze into the hot still room. In the distance, a coyote yipped. Caesar A. growled out in the yard. Trevor slid his tender body into the narrow single bed. Six a.m. would come too soon. Rise and shine. He hoped he'd be able to move in the morning. He was asleep before he could think another thought.

Cool hands massaged Trevor's limbs, his skin slippery with oil. Warm lips on his, moist breath against his cheek. Another dream. Trevor pulled the dream woman's body down on top of his. Dreams have their advantages, he mused, as he drifted back into sleep with a smile on his face.

Trevor awoke as the sky was flushing pink in the east. He was pushed up to the wall; Angela curled against his back, the smell of lavender in the air. He rolled over, grimacing with pain and propped himself on his elbow to look at her. She shifted in sleep and a soft animal moan sounded in the back of her throat. He recalled the feel of a warm ball of fluff in his hands and the rough wet rasp of a tongue on his cheek when he held it to his face. But where was the memory from? Aunt Gladys didn't allow pets. He brushed back a wisp of hair from Angela's forehead. She looked so peaceful, the sharp angles smoothed away by sleep. How little he knew about her. And she about him. They had constructed the rules and thick walls of concrete between them. Last night, in the pages of Helen's photo album, he caught a glimpse of the real Angela, the one who fed a puppy with a baby bottle and played trombone in the school band.

He wondered what he looked like when asleep.

"Hey," he whispered and jiggled her shoulder. She sighed and forced one eye open. "Are you supposed to be here?" he said when he really wanted to suggest they stay in bed all day.

She closed her eye. "It's okay. They never come up here any more."

"Aren't we breaking the rules?"

"You and your stupid rules," she mumbled.

"My rules?" he protested. "I thought they were *our* rules."

"All yours." She rolled onto her back, eyes still closed.

"What about that night I asked you to stay?"

"Lawyer's cardinal rule. Always be suspicious of a sudden change of behaviour." She slipped her head under his arm and planted a kiss on his breastbone. "What time is it?"

He squinted at the clock on the desk. "Five thirty."

She rolled on top of him. "Good, we've got half an hour."

"Ouch," was all he said.

The lone male coyote sat beside a stone cairn at the top of a low hill. He raised his muzzle to the fading stars and howled into the pale dawn sky. He listened for an answering call from his mate, then howled a second time to warn the young male he had encountered earlier to keep his distance. The wide prairie swallowed up his song. He padded down the hill toward the cabin at the edge of the coulee. His shoulders were stiff, his coat ragged, but he was strong and diligent, and had attracted a female for his seventeenth year. He stopped frequently to urinate—the cairn, a scrubby sagebrush, the edge of the trail, a fencepost—all the while his keen nose alert for the reek of another.

He skirted downwind along the edge of a ground squirrel colony. His nose twitched, one ear upright and forward, the other bent and tattered from an old injury. He sat and watched the first fingers of sun stretch slowly across the burrow-riddled earth, light tracing the edges of the shadowy openings he knew bore prey. He crouched low and waited. Ten minutes, fifteen. A small brown head popped up at the entrance to a burrow, sunlight reflecting off the hair on its neck. A second head appeared on the far side of the colony. The body of the coyote tensed. A third ground squirrel emerged fully not four body lengths away and sat upright on its haunches, sniffing the air. The coyote slunk forward on his belly until he could see the whiskers on the animal's nose. He pounced; his paws came down on fur and flesh. He gripped the head in his jaw and bit down. The bone cracked as it gave. The rodent convulsed once and was eaten in two swallows.

A sentinel ground squirrel whistled a warning, and the animals dropped into their burrows one by one. The coyote dug at an entrance, but with little enthusiasm, then urinated down the hole. He loped from the colony, tail relaxed and drooping lazily behind. On nights when hunting proved difficult, he might prowl around the distant farm buildings and search for mice or chickens, but the place smelled of caution, and he was no longer a match for the barking dog.

The pups, six weeks old, yelped at play in the old badger hole which the female had enlarged for her whelping den. It was hidden by a swag of willow. The male drank from the stream and sat a respectable distance from the den. When he huffed, the female's head appeared at the den entrance. She wriggled out and gambolled down the bank to him. Whining with excitement, she licked at his mouth and pawed at his shoulder. He huffed again and at his invitation, five pups squirmed from the mouth of their home and tumbled over one another down the slope to their father. They licked frantically at his muzzle and he regurgitated the prairie dog onto the ground. The puppies set upon the glistening pile of flesh and disjointed bone, growling and jostling one another as they ate. After their meal, their father spread his length out on the earth and let the pups clamber across his body. He was patient for a while, ignoring the nips and swats, but when he'd had enough, he shook himself free and with one backward glance at his female, disappeared to find a quiet place to nap.

FIFTEEN

❦ Angela invited him to the farm again the next weekend. Saturday, after a long day of hoisting bales in heat that crackled, the family drove out to the Swede Lake reservoir, speedboat in tow and a picnic in the back of the truck. The vehicles bumped through arid prairie uplands, yellow and burgundy with prickly pear and cushion cactus. A half dozen long-billed curlews scurried across the road and between the cacti. The land supported few trees; the prairie flowed uninterrupted into the lake. American white pelicans scooped fish from the reservoir with heavy orange bills and took flight en masse in a flurry of wingbeats when Bjorne backed the boat into the water. The hull barely wet, Bjorne fired up the engine and lined the water skis up on the sand beach.

"Let's go," he yelled. "Becca, you ride shotgun." His eleven-year-old daughter hopped into the boat, her flowered bathing suit faded and worn, and took up position in the back seat to report fallen skiers and relay hand signals.

"Guests first," Helen said.

Everyone looked at Trevor. He gawked at the row of fat fibreglass water skis. He didn't want to admit he couldn't swim. "I'm up for a beer. I'm beat," he said with what he hoped was nonchalance.

"Angie," Bjorne yelled, revving the engine and paying out tow line into the shallows. "Come on."

Angela leaned over and touched Trevor's arm as she passed him. "You go next?" She put on a lifejacket, walked into the lake and slipped on a ski. Trevor hurried over and picked up the second ski from the beach to hand to her, but before he could take another step, she grabbed the passing tow bar, effortlessly tucked one foot behind the other and sped away on a single ski.

Trevor's mouth fell open as he watched her skim expertly over the rippled surface, spray cascading behind. The audience on shore clapped and cheered.

"Bjorne skis barefoot," Nancy said, shading her eyes from the sun with her hand. "But not this summer."

"Barefoot?" Trevor couldn't imagine it. "Doesn't it hurt?"

"Only when the water's dead flat. Too much friction." Luke skipped a wedge-shaped stone across the water. "He's teachin' me."

Helen handed Trevor a lawn chair and a beer and he sat beside the truck with Nancy, Helen and Axel while Jake paddled in the weeds at the lake's edge. Angela glided in to shore and stepped confidently out of the binding and onto the beach, her hair still dry.

"Your turn next." She walked past Trevor to the cooler and pulled out a beer.

"Let Luke go," Trevor answered. "He's gonna pee his pants if he waits much longer."

"Thanks man." Luke ran for the water, the muscles in his legs like carved wood.

When Trevor deflected a third invitation with the excuse he had had too much beer, Angela wrinkled up her nose and invited Luke for a double ski. The two cut slalom across each other's wake for twenty minutes. Nancy skied next, then Becca—the only family member who skied using two feet. Jake climbed into Trevor's lap and leaned back, his wet body cool on Trevor's stomach. Trevor didn't know what to do with his hands, he'd never had a child on his lap before. After a moment of indecision, he rested his fingertips on Jake's shoulders and was struck by the softness of his skin and the fact the boy tilted his head back in response and beamed up at him. Jake's eyes were the same colour as Bjorne's.

By this time, two more families had arrived with their boats and the evening turned into a party, food and drink flying as fast as the boats. After supper, Bjorne took Axel and Helen out in the boat for a slow circle around the lake. Once his parents settled back into their lawn chairs, Bjorne signalled to Angela, who lined up on shore with Luke, Becca and three of their friends. The single boat towed the six skiers in parallel formation out onto the lake. The skiers paired up; one of each pair dropped their skis, stepped onto the back of their partner's skis, and climbed up onto their shoulders. Trevor watched in awe as the three pairs skied in so close to one another they were able to join hands between them to form two tiers of three bodies each. He held his breath as Becca clambered up from the middle tier onto Luke's and Angela's shoulders to complete a pyramid.

"How do they do that?" he said.

"Practice," Helen answered.

Trevor whistled and clapped with everyone else on shore as the pyramid executed a graceful circuit of the lake, then sank, laughing, into the shallows near the beach. Trevor wanted to jump up and run down to hug them all, but Jake had fallen asleep in his lap.

Later, as they packed up the truck in the glow of the sunset to go back to the farm, Angela handed him a cooler and said, "You could have said you didn't ski."

"I didn't want to show you up," he joked. "Beside, you built the Great Pyramid."

"How did you manage to get Jake on your lap?" she waggled her finger at him. "We were plotting to throw you in." She whirled and signalled Luke, who raised a thumb to three of his friends. The four teenagers surrounded Trevor, removed the cooler from his hands and dragged him to the lake. As he soared through the air and landed with a smack beyond the weeds, he prayed the water wasn't over his head.

Trevor slept most of the next weekend, recovering from a sales trip, but he and Angela started to help at the farm whenever they had time, leaving Friday after work and driving back Sunday night or early Monday morning. Angela slipped into his room each night after dark when the rest of the household was asleep. One Friday, they arrived to find the single bed from Angela's room had been moved into Trevor's and the beds made up as a double, a vase of black-eyed Susans on the dresser. The next morning at breakfast, Helen shovelled a mound of scrambled eggs onto their plates and said," I hope you two are using precautions."

Angela squeezed her mother's shoulder. "I'm almost thirty-two, Ma."

"Lord knows that's what I'm worried about." Helen forked two extra pieces of bacon onto Trevor's plate.

An easy comradeship evolved between Trevor and Bjorne. Bjorne showed him how to use the farm machinery: the forklift, the tractor, the mower, the combine. Trevor rode along in the truck to check and move the irrigation pipes or to haul feed to the cattle. They talked hockey as they bounced across the fields in the Ford. Bjorne never mentioned his heart problems. Trevor knew from Angela that he was scheduled for heart surgery in late October, after harvest.

In the middle of July, Bjorne commandeered Angela and Trevor to accompany him to pick up a bull from a farm in southern Saskatchewan. The three crowded together in the cab of the five-ton truck with a bag lunch from Helen big enough to last a week. They drove south, Angela sandwiched between the two men. They shared jokes and listened to music. The land grew increasingly bare and flat the further south they went. Near the Saskatchewan border, extensive seasonal sloughs stretched out on either side of the road, the tarmac a curving ribbon floating on a broad shallow lake. Massive flocks of red-capped sandhill cranes foraged on stick legs; canvasbacks and pintails bobbed along, feeding in skittish congregations. At the approach of the truck, the birds ran across the water en masse and took flight, wheeling in great, noisy clouds overhead. Slanting columns of rain approached from the east, and the wind picked up across the expanse of water. White-topped wavelets smacked the roadside. Gusts rocked the truck, threatening to blow it from the road into the water-filled ditch. When the rainstorm hit, Bjorne pulled over, the drops so thick and heavy on the windshield they couldn't see out. They yelled to one another over the din on the metal roof, the atmosphere in the truck intimate and comfortable. Trevor stretched his arm along the seat back behind Angela. He wanted to touch her all the time. He wondered if this was how it felt to be in love.

It took the three of them and the bull's owner an hour to get the belligerent animal into the truck. On the drive home, it snorted and shuffled in the back in spite of sedation.

"Why don't you use artificial insemination?" Trevor asked.

"We like our ladies happy." Bjorne winked at Trevor and nudged Angela who smacked him on the knee. "Hey, Trev, I wrote you a song," he said.

"Me?" Trevor asked. "You wrote me a song?"

"I did. It's a sweet little tune. Too bad I don't have my guitar."

"Sing it anyway," Angela said, smiling at Trevor, who sat tongue-tied in response to the gesture. *Someone wrote him a song?* "What's it called?"

"Not sure yet," Bjorne answered. "It's still a little rough around the edges."

"You're stalling," she protested. "Go on, you can try it out on us."

"You want to hear it, Trev?" Bjorne asked.

"Yeah, of course." Trevor nodded. "You bet."

"Okay, here goes." Bjorne tilted back his cap and started singing, a clear baritone that filled the cab with sound.

This old farm she'll work your fingers to the
bone.
This old farm she'll work your fingers to the
bone.
But I ain't gonna leave her, she's all I got for
home.

Up at dawn, the land won't let me be.
Up at dawn, the land won't let me be.
My body's aching; I'll work until I die.

My baby she loves my tractor more than me.
My baby she loves my tractor more than me.
I'll lose my baby, when my tractor's dead and
gone.

Brother, I got the Swede Lake Tractor Blues.
Brother, I got the Swede Lake Tractor
Blues . . ."

He smacked the steering wheel with the palm of his hand.
"Damn, I just can't come up with that last line."

Angela and Trevor looked at one another and broke out
laughing at Bjorne's expression.

"What are you two so amused about?" He tossed his cap
on the dashboard, his ears and cheeks flushing pink under his
tan.

"I've never seen you embarrassed before," Angela teased.
She leaned over and kissed him on the cheek. "It's fantastic,"
she assured him.

Bjorne swivelled in his seat and stared past her at Trevor.
"I need an unbiased opinion. Trevor?"

Trevor held up his hand and closed his eyes, playing the
tune through in his head. "How about this," he said, then sang

in a faltering tenor. "Brother, I got the Swede Lake Tractor Blues. Brother, I got the Swede Lake Tractor Blues. I'll keep my baby happy, buy her a new John Deere."

Bjorne whistled and Angela cheered. "Perfect. It'll be a hit," Angela crowed, throwing her arms around both their shoulders. "*Swede Lake Tractor Blues* by the unbeatable Bjorne Steffansson and Trevor Wallace."

Trevor didn't think he'd ever been happier in his life.

The storm proved a harbinger of good fortune, and the critical rains arrived on cue. The fields of wheat grew tall and green. The tight pale seed heads promised a successful crop. A mood of contentment and good fortune settled over the farm.

One night after supper in early August, Angela hurried Trevor off the porch before the men could pull him into their regular smoke and talk session.

"Let's go for a drive." She tossed the truck keys from one hand to the other.

They headed past Bjorne's house, through two fences and onto a little used track. Well trained by now, Trevor opened and closed each barbed wire and two-by-four gate along the way. The track narrowed after the second fence, eventually fading to a faint impression in the freshly cut stubble. The truck bumped and jostled to the top of a shallow hill where wheat fields gave way to uncultivated ground. Low grasses and clumps of sagebrush dotted the stony landscape.

"We keep this remnant of shortgrass prairie wild." Angela swept her arm in a wide arc. "Grandpa and Grandma's request. We get a lot of species you don't see much any more. Those purple flowers are lupines. There's a family of burrowing owls about a kilometre north. Next spring, I'll bring you out to see the sage grouse on the booming grounds."

Next spring? Trevor felt a surge of warmth at the prospect

of the future. They'd never made plans together before. He liked the sound of it, a plan to visit some birds . . . next spring. Ahead, the flat plain dropped away into a narrow coulee, a jag of emerald across the prairie, and on the other side, a log cabin perched just back from the edge of the bank.

"That's my grandparents' cabin I told you about." She stopped the truck and turned off the motor.

"Yeah. I remember." He reached out to put his hand on Angela's leg, but she was already sliding out the door. He followed her down a narrow trail into the gully where a fat stream gurgled across rocks and gravel. Side pools of standing water were thick with cattails and bulrushes. Clumps of white fluff from cottonwood in seed floated in the eddies and lined the edges of the stream.

"The water's from an underground spring." Angela explained. "It's the reason this farm exists. It kept my grandparents alive more than one dry summer during the Depression."

They jumped boulders across the stream and climbed the bank to the cabin. The logs were bleached silver from years of weather and gaps showed where the oakum had fallen out. Trevor knocked on an end-cut. "Still solid," he said.

"Granddad knew what he was doing." Angela answered. "The Swedes know how to use their hands." She released the latch and pushed open the door. "I'm the only one who comes here now."

Trevor stepped after her into the single room that must have met all domestic purposes: living room, kitchen, bedroom and, given the dusty chamber pot in the corner, an occasional bathroom. Angela's footsteps echoed on the plank floor. The air smelled of mice droppings. A cast iron wood cookstove and a hand-hewn table dominated the room; a wide bench bordered the back wall and above it a shelf held a flatiron, canning jars and a tin washbasin. Trevor climbed a ladder to the empty loft and sat on the edge, legs dangling. Below him, Angela paused at the picture window in the west wall. The evening sun draped her face and shoulders with light, dust motes swirling in the luminous haze around her. He imagined her a pioneer waiting for her husband to come home from the fields. He dropped from the loft to the floor, and she jumped when he landed with a thump. They both laughed. Across the room, a second window faced the coulee and the grasslands beyond. Trevor wondered if the foothills of the Rockies were visible along the horizon on a crystal-clear day.

"Grandpa brought the glass from Calgary on the back of a buckboard for Gran's thirtieth birthday," Angela said. She ran her fingers down the window, leaving a trail in the dust. "She told me the story a million times. He sold his favourite gun to buy the glass, cut the openings with a hand saw. A gift of sunshine in winter. She cried whenever she told me that story."

Trevor draped his arm around Angela's shoulder. He noticed a nipple-shaped cairn on the top of the next hill to the northwest. It reminded him of a dream he'd had involving an elephant, a night sky, and Constance. He wondered where in the world she might be now? He hoped she was as happy as he.

SIXTEEN

ἦ The first week of September Trevor received another letter from Constance and a bombshell at work. The letter was dated August 11 and from Costa Rica. Trevor pondered the picture for several minutes. Constance leaned over a fence at the edge of a cliff, cloud or a billow of smoke swirling around her. Her left hand pointed out over the chasm, and he wasn't sure whether he read guilt or mischief in her expression.

He propped the photo against the desk lamp and unfolded the sweet-smelling sheet of paper.

August 11
San Jose, Costa Rica

Dear Trevor,

Do you believe in heaven and hell? I recall you told me you weren't religious. I haven't set foot in a church since I left Donald. Here in Costa Rica everyone is Catholic. They all believe in heaven and hell. And purgatory, the waiting place. Horrid stories to frighten little children. If you're good, you'll go to heaven, but if you lie or steal or do bad things, straight to the fires of hell with you. But what if it's true, Trevor? You're fine. All those wonderful things you do for the poor with your tractors. I know those parts you sent to Michael have helped. You are honest and sincere. And helpful to senior citizens. If heaven exists, you'll shoot straight to God's right hand.

But me. I'm damned for what I've done today. I dropped Donald into a volcano. And it was no accident. I took a bus up to the Poas volcano outside San Jose, walked up to the edge of the crater and tossed him in, peanut butter and all. Into a lake of sulphuric acid. Fire and brimstone. I suppose the bottom of a volcano is close enough to hell. I asked a nice American girl I met on the bus to take a picture of the deed but she missed the act. You'll just have to take my word for it.

It's all a mystery isn't it, Trevor? Where we go when we die. But does it matter? Isn't the way we live our lives the important thing? In the end, we're all in the hands of Anubis.

Love, Constance

P.S. Angela's bound for heaven too, with a name like that.

Trevor picked up the picture again. So Constance found a suitable grave for Donald. The bugger deserved it. Her reference to Africa needled at his conscience. Well, he would go right down south with Donald to bask in the fires of hell with his lies and deceit. She thought he was a nice guy. Kind acts for the poor.

Aunt Gladys and Uncle Pat had taken Brent and Trevor to the Lutheran church every Sunday, where they squirmed and fidgeted and played word games with the bulletin until Aunt Gladys smacked them. At fourteen Brent stole money from the offering plate, and Uncle Pat pulled out the stick when they got home. Brent challenged his uncle to a fist fight and when the man lost, he used the event as an excuse to stay home himself. Aunt Gladys dragged Trevor along with her until he also turned fourteen, when she gave up and left them all at home. Uncle Pat drank beer in front of the television, while Brent and Trevor wandered the streets of Regina until lunch, ignoring the list of chores Aunt Gladys had posted on the fridge, knowing they would get the strap.

Trevor clipped the photo to the fridge; the expression on

Constance's face was definitely more mischief than guilt.

The next day when he arrived at work he found a message on his desk to see Andy. He rapped on Andy's office door.

"Come in," Andy called and pushed back his chair. "Trevor," he said. "Sit down."

"What's up?" Trevor said. "Where to?"

Andy opened a file and frowned. "I didn't call you in here to talk schedule." He rotated the file to face Trevor. "Your sales records for the past few months. You're down in every category, Trev. What's going on with you?"

Trevor straightened. "There's a mistake. You're missing paper work."

Andy shuffled through the sheaf. "No. They're all here. Thirteen trips since February. You're down thirty percent. Damn it. Tanzania. They ordered two tractors. Their usual is ten. What happened?"

Trevor swallowed hard and slid down in his chair. "I . . . don't know," he lied. He had merely suggested to the Tanzanian government representative they might be better off with hand ploughs. He knew by the unhealthy red of Andy's face that the information would not be appreciated.

"You don't know?" Andy loosened his tie with one hand.

"I . . . don't." He also mentioned they might want to take advantage of their manpower. "No. Don't know."

Andy slid one hand down his face and across his chin, as if trying to smooth away his anger, then spoke in a tightly controlled voice. "Maybe you need some time to figure out why. Take a break. Are you overworked . . . stressed? Problems at home?"

"I'm fine."

Andy slapped his palm on the folder. "These aren't fine. Take a month off. Get your head straightened around, or whatever you need to do."

"A month off?" Trevor choked.

"Yeah. A month. Starting today." Andy waved his hand toward the door and picked up another file, not bothering to say goodbye when Trevor walked out of the room.

Trevor's head spun as he collected a few things from his desk. Thirty percent down? He had merely suggested his clients pursue less expensive options for a change. Make good use of their human resources. He left a message with the receptionist that he'd be away until October. At the front entrance, he paused, then turned and bounded the stairs two at a time down to the Parts and Service department. He banged on the service bell repeatedly. Sid sauntered out of the warehouse, glasses pushed back on his head. "Hang on, what's your hurry?"

"Sid." Trevor offered his best abandoned-salesman smile.

"Trevor, good to see you. What can I do for you today?"

Trevor rifled through his wallet and handed Sid a crumpled piece of paper. "Would you send a couple of starters and the rest of these parts for the IH 1066 to this address? Charge the bill to my account."

Sid raised his eyebrows as he read and let out a prolonged whistle. "If I can get 'em. Whatever you say boss," he chuckled. "It's your nickel."

"Thanks." Trevor slapped the man on the shoulder across the counter. "You're a pal."

Trevor moped around the apartment for three days. He hadn't taken time off in years. He cleaned house, took long runs down in Fish Creek Park every day, but by evening he was restless and bored. The weekend at the farm was a relief, but he was too embarrassed to tell anyone about his forced vacation, even Angela, who spread out her own work at the kitchen table each night after supper cleanup.

By Wednesday of the second week, he couldn't bear the apartment any longer and drove aimlessly through Calgary until he found himself heading west toward Bragg Creek and Kananaskis on Highway 22X. Cowboy country, the foothills of the Rockies. He stopped at the top of a rise, stepped from the car and leaned against the trunk, the foothill landscape spread out before him. Like liquid, the calm prairie gathered into restless hills under his feet, and swept west to crest like a frozen ocean wave into white-foamed mountain peaks. What was he searching for? Was his head messed up like Andy suggested?

Thursday he drove the highway toward Banff. He turned off at Cochrane and continued out along the Ghost River Valley. At 1,500 metres, the fall air was crisp and an early dusting of snow topped the mountain range. He parked and wandered along the road to a viewpoint over the valley. Trees and mountains blocked the way, and his lungs tightened when he realized he couldn't see the sky. A white-faced steer wandered over to the fence and bawled at him. "Fuck off." Trevor yelled and headed back to the car.

Friday morning he headed north toward Edmonton, drab depressing fence-bound country pocked with oil pumps. He abandoned a vague plan to drive all the way to Edmonton and turned around before Red Deer. At the outskirts of Calgary, where new subdivisions spilled out over the prairie like an invasionary wave, he felt an uncanny pull to the south. Towards what? What was out there for him? Swede Lake? He stopped at a gas station and called Angela.

"You not working?" she asked.

"Andy made me take a couple days off," he said. "Want to go to the farm?"

"I can't get away until the weekend, but go without me," she suggested. "They can always use the help."

He arrived after supper to find Helen at the house with Rachel and Jake. "The rest of them are out harvesting with two of our neighbours," she announced. "You're just in time," she said, as if his appearance was nothing out of the ordinary. "We can use another driver." She shooed him into the house for leftovers, then drove him out to the south quarter where three combines slowly circled the field in unison. Rivers of seeds spit in hissing streams into the back of the grain trucks that followed along beside. Helen signalled for them to stop as they rounded the curve near the truck.

Bjorne jumped down out of the cab of one of the machines and ran up, a smile spread across his face. "Look who's here," he said and clapped Trevor on the back. "You here to work?"

Trevor nodded.

"Let's go then."

Bjorne gave Trevor a refresher on combine operation. "Just follow the guy in front of you, one cut-width over."

"You're leaving me alone?" Trevor said nervously, eyeing the numerous knobs, levers and buttons.

"I don't trust just anyone with my combine," Bjorne said. "You'll do fine. I need to bring on another truck." He climbed down to the ground and turned as he strode away. "See you later."

Later was an understatement. They worked until well after midnight, with a single break for sandwiches and coffee that Helen brought out in the pickup. The headlights shone into the night like beacons, illuminating the sea of ripe wheat ahead. Trevor couldn't relax, his body tense and alert. He didn't want to make a mistake, run into the combine in front of him, the truck beside, flip the wrong lever at the wrong time. The big machine vibrated beneath him and he strained to follow the path of the headlights ahead. He was relieved when they finished the field and Bjorne and Nancy drove him back to the house for a few hours sleep.

"Pick you up at four-thirty," Bjorne said as he let an exhausted Trevor out at Helen's.

They worked fourteen hours straight the next day and by dusk finished the last of the Steffansson's harvest. Helen and the other wives served up a banquet out on the front lawn on tables bowed with the weight of the food. Trevor admired the easy camaraderie of the farm people as they joked among one another, amid a background of domestic chatter, and shared their concerns about the predicted rain showers. They paid no attention to the spectacular swath of pink and purple in the western sky from the setting sun, not because of indifference, but because they were part of the whole. Tomorrow, they'd move the combining operation to the next farm, and the next, working through the night again if they had to, until all the crops were in. Trevor watched Nancy with Jake in her arms serve dessert to Bjorne, who curled his arm affectionately around his wife's waist in response. The intimacy made him think of Angela; he was surprised to realize he missed her.

He cleared his dishes from the table, but before he reached the kitchen, Bjorne cut him off at the porch. "When you've finished with the women's work, Trev, meet me at the truck. Time to celebrate," he whispered and sauntered away like he'd spent the day lounging by a pool instead of driving a hot dusty truck since before dawn. Trevor wanted more than anything to sneak up to bed to rest in preparation for another long day on the combine tomorrow and the drive back to Calgary. He held up the dirty plates and utensils in his hands. Women's work. He delivered the dishes through the screen door and headed out to the garage.

Bjorne leaned against the cab; a cigarette dangled from the corner of his mouth.

"Atta boy." He held up a thumb in approval. "I'll have you trained out of those bad habits soon enough." He opened the door of the truck. "Hop in."

"Where to?" Trevor asked. What was it about him that

made people enjoy lassoing him in for unexpected journeys?

Bjorne tossed his hat behind the seat and smoothed his hair. "To the centre of the universe."

"The centre of the universe?"

"Yup, the Swede Lake Hotel."

From the top of the hill about a mile from Swede Lake, the town appeared little more than a cluster of trees across the railway tracks from three grain elevators. And truth be known, Swede Lake consisted of no more than a few unpaved streets alongside the railway tracks and three grain elevators. A church, a school, the fire hall, a curling rink and, to his surprise, an ancient White Rose station that appeared to still be in operation. Bjorne drove down Centre Street, the commercial block and a half that bisected the community. It felt like a ghost town. At the corner of Centre Street and First Street, he pulled up in front of the Swede Lake Hotel, a boxy clapboard gold and white building right out of a Western movie. A few dusty trucks were parked outside. Trevor was disappointed not to find swinging saloon doors at the entrance to the building. Inside, the dimly lit tavern smelled of stale beer and cigarettes. A stand-up bar ran along the back of the room. A large jar of pickled eggs and another of beef jerky on the countertop were reflected in the long back mirror on the wall below a collection of liquor bottles lined up along a high shelf. A staircase, with a sign *Rooms for Rent*, led to a second floor. Three men sat at the bar. Country music twanged from a vintage juke box.

Bjorne and Trevor sat at one of the round tables, the varnished wooden top etched with names and cigarette burns. Bjorne signalled the bartender, who arrived a moment later with a tray of draft beer glasses which he arranged on the table in front of them. Bjorne downed his first glass in one swig and wiped his hand across his mouth. "That should wash away an hour's worth of prairie dust. Thirteen more to go."

He handed a beer to Trevor and picked up a second for himself, flourishing it in the air. "Here's to the making of a farmer." He winked at Trevor and drained the glass.

"I don't know about that."

"No, you're a natural. It's in your blood." Bjorne pulled a package of smokes from his shirt pocket and offered one to Trevor.

"No thanks. I thought you were quitting."

"Nah, that's what I tell Ma to get her off my back." Bjorne lit his cigarette and shook the match. A wisp of smoke trailed from the end. "You ever smoke?"

"My brother dared me into smoking a pack on my fifteenth birthday. Let's say it did me in for life." If Trevor remembered correctly, Brent had doubled over in gales of laughter as Trevor vomited onto the street.

"Fair enough. I started at eight. String, grass and whatever else we could find. I guess I was a natural too." He inhaled another long drag, the end of the cigarette flaring red. "I should quit. Nancy and Ang are always on my case." He pushed back his chair. "This music's gotta go."

He sauntered over to the juke box, fishing change out the back pocket of his jeans, then dropped in a coin and pressed a couple of buttons. The Rolling Stones singing *Honky Tonk Women* replaced the western twang.

"That's better. We're not country hicks out here in the boonies," he said as he sat down and chugged another glass of beer. "Once we're finished this damn harvest, we can get on with the real work."

"The real work?"

"Yeah, hockey season."

Hockey talk carried them through the beer and into the hard liquor: rye and Coke for Bjorne, scotch for Trevor.

Trevor quit wondering why Bjorne invited him to the Swede Lake Hotel and settled into the easy sociability of the evening. Bjorne reminded him of Brent. Happy go lucky, daring, the world by the tail, even when the tail burned like the fuse on a stick of dynamite. Bjorne avoided any talk of his heart attack and the scheduled surgery. His tanned face radiated health. Trevor saw no indication the man was sick, in fact, he felt like an invalid beside Bjorne Steffansson.

By ten o'clock most tables were taken, the room thick with cigarette smoke.

"Quiet night." Bjorne yelled over the din.

"Quiet?" Trevor yelled back.

"Most Saturday nights you can't move in here. Everybody's harvesting." The men soon tired of having to yell to talk and their conversation dwindled to drink orders. People stopped by to greet Bjorne. They patted him on the back, or shook his hand while they talked about the weather or asked how harvest was proceeding. Bjorne introduced Trevor to each and every one as his friend. At midnight, Bjorne slapped Trevor on the shoulder and tilted his head toward the door. "We gotta work early tomorrow."

Outside a ball of orange filled the eastern sky.

"Damn. Harvest moon," Bjorne drawled. "Good luck's a-comin'."

Trevor staggered along behind Bjorne, amazed the man walked as if he'd been guzzling soda pop all night. The music from the bar followed them down the street. Bjorne unbuckled his belt, eased down his zipper and peed at the side of the road. Trevor followed suit; the two streams of hot liquid hissed into the grass. Trevor swayed like a stalk of wheat in the wind.

"You're a good shit, Trevor," Bjorne said. "I don't know what you're waiting for. Ask her."

"Ash her?" Trevor slurred. "Ash who?"

"Angie. Ask her to marry you. She's dying for it."

"She is?" Trevor's head spun. He wasn't even used to the idea of having her for an official girlfriend. Marriage wasn't on the radar screen. At least, not before tonight.

"Sure, I can tell. She's my baby sister, isn't she?"

Bjorne shook off, zipped up and headed down the road in the opposite direction of the truck. Trevor tucked himself in and hopped after Bjorne as he fumbled with his fly.

"But the truck's that way." As Trevor turned to point back at the hotel, he tripped over his own feet, and sprawled in the dust.

Bjorne hauled Trevor up from the dirt. "Can't take your liquor? Thought you were a farm kid." He gripped Trevor's shoulders from behind and propelled him down the street, across the school field, and up to an oval skating rink surrounded by a waist-high wall of dilapidated boards.

"You told me you played defence," Bjorne said. "I wanna see how good you are."

"No ice," Trevor managed, swaying slightly when Bjorne released him. "No skates."

"No problem." Bjorne palmed a rock from the ground, then disappeared behind the corner of a rickety shed beside the rink. He returned carrying two battered hockey sticks, the blade split on one, black tape trailing from the handle of the other, faded red letters spelling CCM visible along the shaft. "These'll do." He offered them to Trevor. "Left or right?"

"Huh?" Trevor said, Bjorne's intention finally dawning on his drink-addled brain.

"Do you play left-handed or right-handed?" Bjorne asked again, and clapped the two blades together with a crack.

"Right, I think?" Had he admitted to playing defence? If he had, it was another fib. Most of his hockey experience, other than the occasional skirmish back in Regina with Brent and his friends on the road or the pond in the park, took place in the penalty box, mittened hands in his pockets for extra warmth, keeping his brother company after Brent's latest fight with the opposition. Not that he hadn't wanted to play, but Uncle Pat said one broken-nosed brawler in the house was enough. A loyal fan, however, he knew the rules of the game, and when Bjorne shoved the stick into his hands and vaulted over the fence, he felt a rush of exhilaration. He heaved himself across the boards, only to find himself straddled midway. He teetered there for a precarious moment before rolling inside onto the concrete.

"Are you shit-faced or what?" Bjorne yelled from the middle of the rink, where he crouched ready to drop the rock on the faded centre line. "I'm gonna skin you like a rabbit."

Trevor staggered over and faced Bjorne, who pointed behind Trevor where the outline of the goal crease was as faint as the middle line. "Anything in the crease is a goal." Trevor leaned forward, using his stick for support, mimicking the stance he recalled from years of observing Brent. Like Bjorne, Brent played centre forward.

The two men stared each other down for what felt like an eternity. Trevor shook his head to still Bjorne's face, which wobbled and split into threes if he stared too long. He raised the blade of his stick to meet Bjorne's. Bjorne tapped Trevor's stick once with his, and then dropped the misshapen excuse for a puck. Before Trevor could move, Bjorne snatched the rock and ran down the rink, playing the puck back and forth with the face of his stick.

"Steffansson breaks away, he skates down the ice, he shoots, he scores!"

The rock clattered through the goal crease and bounced off the backboard with a thonk. Bjorne paraded around the rink, stick raised high above his head.

Trevor swayed at centre ice, dazed. "Hey, not fair," he called.

Bjorne trotted past and patted Trevor's leg with the

blade of his stick. "You're right. You play defence."

Bjorne ran circles around Trevor for half an hour, scoring one goal after another. Finally, Trevor sobered enough to steal the puck from Bjorne's stick. He headed to the opposite end of the rink. Bjorne came up behind and banged his stick on the concrete.

"If you weren't my future brother-in-law, I'd whup your ass good."

Trevor readied for a slapshot on the goal, but before his stick had completed half its arc, Bjorne reached between Trevor's legs, scooped the rock backwards with the blade, and ran.

"Goal," he yelled from the other end of the rink.

Trevor threw his stick to the ground. The wooden handle cracked in two. He snatched up the pieces and charged after Bjorne, brandishing the broken halves in the air. "I'll kill you Steffansson."

"High sticking," Bjorne yelled.

Trevor threw himself at the man, knocking him to the pavement. "Got you," he crowed.

Bjorne didn't reply. Trevor rolled off his friend's chest and sat back on his heels. Bjorne was red-faced and grunting, curled into a ball.

"Hey buddy." Trevor reached out and touched him on the shoulder. "You all right?"

Bjorne continued to grunt, but when Trevor leaned forward to support him, he raised his hand. "I'm . . . fine," he gasped. "Lost my air."

A moment later, Bjorne unrolled from his fetal position and stretched out onto his back. Trevor was relieved when the man's breath evened out and the colour of his face more closely approximated his usual ruddy glow. Trevor flopped down on his back beside him.

"Sure you're okay?" Trevor asked again.

"Right as rain," Bjorne answered, his voice back to normal.

"Shit, I shouldn't have said that." He pointed up.

Clouds had obscured the saucer moon and the canopy of stars, brilliant an hour ago, were gone. Two wet drops splashed onto Trevor's forehead, and Bjorne breathed out slowly. "Guess that's game."

They hurried back to the truck. The wind rose as they ran, whipping their loose shirttails around their waists. Before they could climb inside the cab, the sky opened and unleashed a deluge.

Bjorne groaned. "Fuck it. Hey, God, hold off with the rain for a few more days."

They drove north out of town toward the farm. The wipers thwacked across the windshield at full speed to keep up with the downpour. Bjorne hunched over the steering wheel in order to see the road. When they passed a broken-down gate that marked the halfway mark home, he started to sing. "This ole farm she'll work ya to the bone." Trevor joined in, the wipers keeping time like a metronome. "But I can't leave her, she's all I got for home." The glow of the dashboard lights illuminated Bjorne's face. At that moment, Trevor wanted nothing more than to be this man's brother. To stay on the farm forever and cuddle up in bed with Angela every night. He could stay. He had nothing to go back to Calgary for. An empty apartment. No job.

"Ask her." Bjorne's head bobbed with the music.

Trevor waved his arms with the beat and bellowed out, "My baby she loves my tractor more than me."

The next morning his resolve dissolved like the aspirins he took for his pounding headache. As if in answer to Bjorne's midnight prayer, the night rain had missed the neighbour's farm, and they were able to combine for half a day before a steady downpour set in. Trevor guzzled water, unable to eat. Before supper, he invented the prospect of an upcoming sales trip and drove back to Calgary.

SEVENTEEN

❦ Monday morning Trevor slept late. His stomach had not recovered from the Saturday night overdose of alcohol. He forced down cereal and strong coffee and decided on another drive. A run was out; he didn't trust his legs to hold. He drove south to Okotoks, then west toward the foothills, taking random turns at inconspicuous intersections. On a narrow gravel road out back of Millarville, he noticed a For Sale sign on a property. *80 Fertile Acres. House and Good Well.* He parked the car in the rutted driveway and swung open the rusted metal gate, which squealed on its hinges. The house appeared abandoned, most of the windows broken. A half dozen roof shingles flapped in the wind. He jiggled the door against the rusted padlock but surprisingly it held. Behind the house, he waded through a sea of knee-high grass and dandelions to a battered picnic table and sat down. The house wasn't much, a single floor and dilapidated, but the view was spectacular, the Rockies far enough away to give the sky room. Open prairie to the east and south. He should buy a place like this. Quit flying around the world and settle down to a farming life. A good life. Healthy, useful. Your own boss. He didn't know much about farming, only what Bjorne had taught him in a few months of weekends. He supposed the land here would support cattle, wheat better suited to the flatter country. Angela would know what to do. Bjorne and Axel, masters of all trades, could give him a hand. He lay back on the table. Clouds swirled in the sky above him: lambs and bunnies, another that reminded him of a warrior on a horse. On lazy summer days when Aunt Gladys wasn't home, he cloud-watched with Brent on the roof. They invented stories about the cloud people and how they would swoop down one day and rescue them from Regina. Today he needed rescuing from Calgary, from himself. He watched a dragonfly trace a triangular pattern above him, and fell asleep on the picnic table.

As he left the property an hour later, he noted down the number of the realtor. He would bring Angela out for a look. They could miss a weekend in Swede Lake, use a little time alone. He pictured them fixing up the house together. Paint, mend the roof. He could rent a Rototiller and make her a garden. She would can him green beans.

It was dark by the time he arrived at the city limits, Calgary a sea of lights. He headed toward Angela's place, a lower suite in a house in Strathcona. She could afford a house of her own; God knows what she did with all her money. Donations to charities and street people? He had a sudden impulse to help the less fortunate. Volunteer at the food bank. Write out a cheque to one of those insistent organizations that mailed him appeals for money: the Cancer Society, World Vision. He stopped at the corner store to buy Angela a bouquet of flowers. He had never bought flowers for anyone before; he wandered up and down the benches of bloom-filled buckets outside the store for ten minutes. Roses too forward. Might scare her away. Mums too formal. He settled on a large bunch of tiger lilies. They would compliment her hair.

When he reached Angela's house, it was all he could do not to run through the garden to the vine-covered door, flowers clutched in one hand. What would she think when she saw the tiger lilies? The old run-down farm. He slowed. Hell, he had to take chances or his life would never change. He'd die a lonely old man like Constance's husband, what was his name? Tommy? *Take chances.* Hadn't Constance said that to him the last time he saw her? He hadn't heard from the elderly woman in a few weeks. He tapped on the door and a moment later Angela opened it, face ashen, hair tousled, eyes red-rimmed.

"Trevor, I've been calling you for hours," she sobbed, unsteady on her feet.

He reached for her. "What's wrong?"

"It's Bo. He's had another heart attack." She collapsed into his arms.

Trevor's throat constricted. The tiger lilies fell forgotten to the floor. His mind flashed to an image of Bjorne's still body on the concrete of the hockey rink. *I'm going to kill you Steffansson.* Trevor's legs trembled under him. He wanted to crumple into a heap on the doorstep, but he couldn't. He was holding Angela up.

September 13, 1985
Sooke, B.C.

Dear Trevor:

I arrived home last week. After I laid Donald to sizzle, I searched Central America and Mexico for a place for Martin. One day at the Mayan ruins of Chichen Itza, the truth hit me. Martin belonged at home, with me. We flew back to Victoria. We went all around the world together, he and I, like we dreamed.

I never did get a chance to tell you all about Martin. We met at the bookstore. He came in every Tuesday to browse the new releases. He bought his *Complete Works of William Shakespeare* from me. We talked books on Tuesdays, which became lunch after a few months. We began as friends and became lovers.

I have a confession to make. Martin and I never married. We lived in sin for those years at Salal Cottage. We never could see the point of marrying. We loved each other and that's what mattered. I lied to my children, though; the truth would have scandalized them.

Martin fed my soul. We talked about everything. He taught me the names of the plants and animals that lived in the forest on our land: the pink fawn lilies along the stream in spring, the tiny saw-whet owls, the banana slugs. He read me poetry at night. Cooked me wonderful meals and rubbed my feet when my arthritis acted up. He'd take me out in the bay in our rowboat and tell me Native legends about the sea. We walked barefoot on beaches and splashed around in the tidepools like children.

Martin once told me the coastal Natives used to lay out their dead in canoes in the trees, or in caves along the shore. I scattered him in the stream that runs behind Salal Cottage, where the salmon will spawn and die in November. Under the Douglas firs and the maidenhair fern. He flowed out to the sea, but I can feel him here beside me. He taught me to love.

I hope you might come and visit me Trevor. I've noted my phone number at the bottom of the page. I won't travel again for the next while. I've been gone much too long and I'm tired.

Say hi to Angela.

Love Constance

250-633-4187

The coyote pup was curled in the grass behind a clump of sage as if asleep but when the male sniffed and nudged her with his nose, the body, though warm, rolled limply to the side. The adult coyote pawed at the pup's neck but the young animal didn't stir. She hadn't returned to the den with the others after her first independent foray into the world to hunt for mice, and the male set out to find her. An easy task to follow the scent of her siblings. He pawed at her still body again and knew she was gone like so many other pups over the years. Some simply disappeared and never returned, others were snatched by hawks, bitten by badgers or snakes. A few, like this one, were unmarked and bore no foreign scent.

He picked her limp body up in his jaws and dragged her a few steps but she was three-quarters grown and almost as heavy as he, so he dropped her into the brittle grass and licked at her mouth, whining. A vulture swung overhead and the male growled, a deep internal rumble. He paced widening circles around the spot, marking shrubs and boulders as he went, then returned a few strides from her stiffening body and settled down on the ground to wait.

EIGHTEEN

W "Ashes to ashes. Dust to dust," the minister recited from the prayer book. His black cassock fluttered in the prairie wind. Eight men lowered two caskets into the hole. Young Trevor squirmed, his hand sweaty in Aunt Gladys's grip. He wanted to walk over to the hole and look for a bottom. Or watch to see if the wooden boxes would drop straight down into the fires of hell. He wanted to yell to the people in the cemetery, the women who wept into their lace handkerchiefs, the men staring, stern and solemn, into space. Everyone in black.

He wanted to yell, "It wasn't their fault."

But the evidence of his parents' sins stood right in front of the mourners: two young boys, in miniature black suits and ties, their hair slicked back with Aunt Gladys's spit, who pressed her icy fingers into their shoulders to hold them still.

Uncle Pat mounded the last spade of earth on top of the graves. The women scattered flowers from the shop in town: white lilies and chrysanthemums and others he didn't know. "Fake flowers," his mother had called them. She always had a vase of prairie wildflowers in the middle of the kitchen table: crocus in spring, buffalo beans, daisy, wild rose and blue flax in summer.

People trailed in silent groups of two or three from the cemetery to the church that stood—a white beacon—at the top of a rounded hill. They ate date squares and sipped tea from china cups, the talk already turned from the misfortune of Trevor's parents to the latest wheat prices and the lack of rain.

Brent grabbed him by the hand and pulled him around to the back of the church. The two boys sat on the wooden swing set and dragged their Sunday shoes in the dirt. Brent ran up the incline of the teeter-totter, straddled his feet across the central support and rocked from side to side until he had balanced the long board in mid-air. He sprang off with a whoop. One end of the teeter-totter slammed onto the ground with a whack and bounced twice. The impact left a deep gouge in the black earth.

The two boys sprawled on the grass at the crest of the hill. Trevor knew they weren't to get their suits dirty and told his brother so. Brent pulled off his jacket and tie and helped Trevor out of his. Brent slung his arm around Trevor's shoulders. The brothers chewed on long whips of spear grass and stared out across the prairie. A ferruginous hawk hunted overhead, screeching for its dinner.

"Watch this." Brent stretched out along the ground, arms over his head, legs squeezed tight. Slowly, he rolled toward the downhill slope. His body gathered speed on the incline, faster and faster; blades of grass bent beneath him and dust kicked up in puffs where his shoes hit the ground. Trevor could see only the intermittent flash of Brent's face and his wheat-blonde hair flipping by. At the bottom of the hill, Brent's body came to a stop. He didn't move.

"Brent?" Trevor's thin high voice wavered from the top of the hill. He hoped his brother wasn't dead. Who would he have then? He almost cried when Brent staggered to his feet, white shirt flapping around his skinny torso, black with dirt, his church pants filthy. He roared like an angry lion and flailed his arms as he charged back up the hill. Dust blew from his clothes, his face grew scarlet. Fire burned in his eyes. Brent reached Trevor and rested his hand on his brother's shoulder. His ribs heaved under the fine cotton of his grimy dress shirt. Trevor's head filled with the pounding of Brent's heart.

Brent picked up two rocks. One he tossed up and down in his left hand; the other he handed to Trevor. Then he walked up to the church and pitched his rock at the white clapboard wall. The stone left a black mark and a dent where it hit, then fell to the ground with a thud. He picked up another the size of a potato and threw it too. A third. He flicked Trevor's arm with his finger.

"You too," he urged.

Trevor looked down at the stone in his hand. It was pink and white, speckled like a bird's egg with silvery chips that glinted in the sun. The stone sat heavy in Trevor's hand. He searched his brother's face for a reason, but found only flames. Did Brent know a secret? Would this bring back his parents? A sin in payment for another sin? For throwing rocks at the church was surely a sin. A trade. The two boys in exchange for their parents. He stepped forward and threw the stone like a baseball, the way Brent taught him in the backyard a summer ago. The impact of the rock on the wall was satisfying, and he searched around for another. He spied a cinnamon-coloured stone as flat as a pancake and picked it up. It was heavier than the speckled one. He threw it with all his strength at the church. Together, the two boys pelted the building again and again. They grunted with the exertion, the siding growing pocked with rock wounds. Their good Sunday shirts grew wet and transparent with sweat, their fervent young bodies shining through.

It wasn't until Brent began to shout curses—words Trevor had never heard before—that the adults noticed and came running. Uncle Pat grabbed them both around the waist and carried them to the front yard of the church. Trevor dangled still and fearful from one arm; Brent kicked and screamed from the other.

But Uncle Pat didn't go to the grave, pull up the fresh black topsoil with his work-callused hands and throw the two boys in. He didn't grin in satisfaction as the brothers dropped like stones into the fires of hell. He didn't brush the dirt from his hands while Trevor and Brent fell down, down, down, nor did their parents, pain and gratitude mingled on their faces, rise like fluffy white clouds from the heat and the musty shadows to pass their sons midway. Instead, Uncle Pat tossed the two boys into the back of his dented Chevy and ordered them to shut up and sit still. Aunt Gladys scolded them for the state of their Sunday best as they sped from the churchyard. Dust spewed from behind the car on the arrow-straight country road.

Trevor and Brent didn't go to hell. They went to Regina.

Angela leaned on Trevor's arm. She wasn't the only person using Trevor for support; it was as if there wasn't enough strength left in the Steffansson family to hold them up. They had all migrated to Trevor during the days before Bjorne's funeral. Two-year-old Jake climbed into Trevor's arms on the walk from the church to the cemetery across the road. Bjorne's wife Nancy, flanked by her two brothers from Lethbridge, could neither speak nor cry. She and the kids would return to Lethbridge with her brothers after the funeral; the moving van had left yesterday, crammed with furniture from the bungalow. Bjorne's brother Matthew, who arrived from Ottawa the day after Bjorne died, held Helen's elbow. The woman fought back tears as she struggled through the hymns: "Onward Christian Soldiers," "Nearer My God to Thee." Axel hadn't spoken for days.

As the casket was lowered into the grave, Trevor had the strange urge to walk over and peer down into the pit. He felt an odd weight in his hand and the grit of dirt between his fingers that made him think of Constance and her ashes, and her descriptions of obscure death rituals in other countries. He couldn't imagine turning Bjorne into ashes. A flicker of motion at the edge of his vision drew his attention and he turned his head to see the bushy tip of a tail disappear behind a tombstone at the edge of the cemetery. Were the scavengers gathering?

The coyotes and the hawks? The dog-headed Egyptian god to accompany Bjorne to the next life? What country was it where Constance said they left bodies in the wilderness for beasts to rip apart and carry off? Angela nudged him and he moved with her into the line of family and friends who, one by one, shuffled past the open grave of Bjorne Steffansson and threw a fistful of soil onto the descending coffin. It was fitting for Bjorne to go into the earth on which he had worked all his life. His good heart as light as a feather.

Trevor squeezed Angela's shoulders and she shifted more of her weight onto him. He had driven her to the Calgary hospital where the ambulance had taken Bjorne. They camped out in the corridors with Helen, Axel and Nancy for the two days Bjorne hung on to life support. They watched helplessly as the spirit drained from their son, brother and husband, the heart attack irreparable, the damage extensive, the hope of surgery lost. Bjorne died at noon on Thursday. One moment breath and a beating heart, the next, nothing.

A windbreak of trembling aspen bordered the cemetery to the south, and the golden leaves rustled in the wind like a multitude of ghostly whisperings from the graves. He missed Bjorne. His friend. How could he be gone? Forty-two years old, the same age as Brent. Trevor couldn't throw off the nagging thought that he was to blame, that their drunken game of hockey had brought on the fatal heart attack. He could have stopped it, talked Bjorne into going home, talked him out of the drinking expedition altogether. But it hadn't crossed his mind. He did not possess the courage to tell Angela; self-reproach sat hard and cold in his stomach like a rock.

After the funeral, a caravan of cars drove back to the farmhouse. Trevor helped make coffee in borrowed percolators and set plates of dessert out on the dining-room table until the women shooed him out of the house. He found Angela with Caesar A. in the garden. She was pulling weeds, the front of her dress stained with mud where she knelt between the rows of carrots and beets. She ripped chickweed and dandelions out in angry fistfuls. The dog tried to lick her face, but she pushed him away.

The right words eluded Trevor. He stooped three rows down and began to pull spikes of plants from the loose well-tilled soil, discarding them in the paths between the rows. Every once in a while he glanced over at Angela, but she continued to work, head down, shoulders hunched over. What would Bjorne have said to a mourning sister? To him. *Go ask her?* But he couldn't, it wasn't the right time or place.

A shadow fell across the row as he grasped a leafy green top with his fist.

"What the hell are you doing?"

He looked up. Angela loomed over him, fingers pressed to her mouth. She swatted the top of his head with a handful of dandelions.

"Weeding?"

"You're pulling out all the parsnips, you fool."

"Whoops." Trevor grimaced, looking down at the plant in his hand. Angela turned away, her laughter now breathless gasps of anguish. Trevor straightened; a pale yellow tuber smeared with mud dangled from one hand. "Angela?"

Her face contorted with hurt and fury. His instinct made him want to turn away. What in his life had prepared him for this role of comforter? He thought of Constance, the fateful meeting at the Frankfurt airport, the sunflower bag, the plastic bottles that held her three painful stories, and still she reached out her hand to him. To help him up. He took Angela's hand and removed the weeds one by one from her fist, uncurled her fingers, and slipped his hand into her muddy palm. "Let's walk."

They wandered through the fields of fall stubble. Broken stalks crunched under their feet. The dog ran ahead, sniffing at shrubs and abandoned gopher holes. The autumn sun had lost most of its heat and the air smelled of pending frost, snow soon to blanket the farm in white drifts. Angela didn't speak until they saw the cabin at the edge of the coulee.

"I'm taking a year's leave," she announced in a breath. "I'm not going back."

Trevor turned her to him and searched her face. "Why?" he asked.

"My parents can't handle the farm alone. Matthew has another life. We're going to sell it. There's a lot to do to get it ready. And I have to find Mom and Dad a place to go."

"No," he said. "You can't."

"But it's impossible. I can't do it alone. We have no choice."

He wanted to ask her why she hadn't discussed this decision with him, a decision a couple should make together. A couple. Angela and Trevor.

"I'll stay," he said, his voice hoarse. "I can work. Axel can teach me what do before winter. I'll fix the machinery. Order seed for next year and what about—"

"You would stay?" she gasped. "But your job?"

Behind Angela's head the cairn on the top of the hill beckoned to him; for a split second he thought he saw the outline of an elephant waiting at the summit. He threw his hands up in the air. "Hell, I hate my job," he yelled and kissed her so hard on the mouth she stumbled for balance when he released her. Trevor charged up the hill to the cairn; the prairie radiated out in all directions. He tilted his head back and howled into the sky like a coyote. To his surprise, a responding cry echoed from the south. At the bottom of the hill, Angela looked on. Behind her in the coulee, the wolf willow and Saskatoon bushes burned with autumn golds and reds.

He cupped his hands around his mouth and proclaimed to the sky, the wide prairie, the earth at his feet, "Faaarrmmer. I'm a friggin' farmer."

The overwhelming urge to lie down on the ground gripped him, and he stretched out on his back. Slowly, he began to roll, over and over down the hill in his black funeral suit, gathering speed as he turned, the toes of his shoes sending clouds of dust into the air.

"You're a crazy man." Angela giggled through tears as he rolled against her feet, his face and clothes filthy with mud and bits of grass. She fell in a heap on top of him.

"No, I'm a crazy farmer." He pulled her against him and nuzzled her ear. "Your farmer."

He loosened the tie at the back of her dress and the row of buttons from neck to waist, then slipped his hands against her warm skin. Caesar A. pranced around them and whined, then settled down a few metres away and chewed on a stick. A red-winged blackbird whistled from the coulee.

Afterwards, Angela leaned back against him on the cabin steps and they watched a V of migrating ducks head south. Most of the birds had left already. Except for the lone blackbird and the murmur of the spring, the coulee was silent.

"I want to live here." Trevor curled a strand of Angela's hair around his finger.

"Here? In the cabin?"

"Right here."

"But there's no power. No running water. You've gone nuts."

"That's okay. Your grandparents managed. And I'll have you to keep me warm. And an incredible view."

Caesar A. sat up, ears erect.

"Hey, look." Angela gestured with her chin and reached for Caesar's collar.

Three coyotes, an old male veteran the size of a small border collie, and two half-grown pups, appeared at the top of the coulee, their coats thick with pre-winter growth. Trevor had imagined they would be bigger; they reminded him of the jackals at the pyramids, the same judgmental stare, the alert upright ears, the eyes that missed nothing. While the adult stood sentry, the pups filed down to the stream and drank, then loped back up the bank to rejoin him. The three headed west toward the farm.

"I wonder if they spied on us out there," Trevor joked.

"A person can't get privacy anywhere round here," Angela said absently, staring after the animals. "Did that old male have a damaged ear?"

"Didn't notice." Trevor leaned forward and whispered into the crease of her neck. "I've got something for you."

He eased out from behind her and climbed the trail down to the spring. He pulled his handkerchief from his pocket and dipped it in the water. Returning to the cabin with the dripping cloth, he went inside and began to wash the years of dust from the west picture window. Angela watched from outside, arms crossed. She shook her head, then lifted up her skirt and pulled off her slip. Like Trevor, she soaked the silky fabric in the stream then positioned herself opposite him, washing the outside of the window in broad circular strokes.

Trevor thought of Bjorne deep in the grave a few miles away and his brotherly advice. The kind Brent would have given him. "Angela?" he called.

"Yes."

"Do you think your firm could help me find my brother Brent?"

She studied his face. "Sure, no problem."

A clear oval of glass grew between them. Angela flattened her face against the pane and stuck out her tongue. More than a dirty window opened between them. For once, he trusted another person to understand him, his troubles diminished to specks of dust on a pane of glass, wiped away with water on a cloth. He rubbed at the upper corner of the window, talking as he worked. The end of his cloth dangled unnoticed, smudging the clean glass below.

"I've been worried," he confessed.

"About what?" Angela mirrored his arm movements.

"I hurt Bjorne last Saturday night in a drunken game of shinny after the bar. I pushed him down and . . . he couldn't breathe. He claimed the fall winded him. But after his heart attack, you know, I wondered if—"

Angela had stopped washing. The dirty slip fell to the porch. Her face blanched. "But you knew . . ." she said, her voice a whisper. "You knew," she shouted. "You knew he was sick. You knew his surgery was in a month. Hockey? You played hockey with him? You stupid, stupid man."

NINETEEN

W Trevor spent Christmas Day in front of the television with a case of beer and the Super Bowl while a blizzard raged outside his apartment. He was tempted to phone the farm but he knew Angela would hang up on him again. The last time he saw her she was splashing across the coulee stream, not bothering to jump the rocks, the bottom of her skirt trailing a line of water up the stream bank.

Trevor searched the half-empty shelves in his fridge, then decided to order Chinese from the takeout in Kensington. As the refrigerator door thumped shut, a magnet clattered to the floor along with a photo. Constance smiled up at him from the linoleum. She wore an oversized man's sweater and a baggy pair of green sweatpants, no wig. Her hair stuck out in eccentric tufts from her scalp. In the letter, she had written that the trip had exhausted her, and when he looked closer at the photo he agreed she appeared tired and lacked her usual sparkle. Behind her, a pretty sky-blue and white cottage, smothered in scarlet and orange-leaved vines, shone like a rainbow. He could picture her in the house with her cats and the memories of her husbands. Suddenly he wanted to talk to her again, his single real friend in the world now that Bjorne was dead and Angela hated him. Maybe he should take a trip west. He'd never seen the coast. And she had invited him to visit, hadn't she? Trevor rummaged around in his desk for her phone number. As he dialled, his mood brightened at the thought of the surprise and pleasure in her voice when she answered. But the phone rang three times before a recorded message broke in to inform him the number was out of service. He tried again with the same result. "This number is no longer in service. Please check the num—"

"Crap," he swore and passed up the chop suey for bed.

Trevor was on a bus. Outside the window, herds of reebok and zebra grazed on the spare grass that grew on a red-dirt land as flat as the Alberta prairie. His mouth tasted of dust. The bus stopped. Trevor edged his way down the crowded aisle and stepped out onto the gravelled road. Someone threw his bag from the overpacked luggage carrier on the roof and it landed with a thud at his feet. He picked it from the dirt, slipped his arms into the straps and walked down a narrow track toward distant huts. The backpack hurt his shoulders. He removed it and opened the drawstring to find tractor parts—three starters, a distributor and a cardboard box of spark plugs. He carried on to the village. People watched from doorways, from gardens. A young man, his white cotton shirt blinding against his black skin, stepped up to him and extended his hand. "Constance said you would come." The man handed Trevor a spear and pointed out into the savannah. "The warriors wait."

A line of ochre-painted youth, also carrying spears, leaped and ululated under an enormous baobab tree. Like a herd of gazelle, they turned in unison and ran east across the dry ground. Trevor ran with them, through masses of animals— giraffe, zebra, gazelle, water buffalo. Without warning, the warriors stopped and formed a circle. Trevor walked through to the middle where he found a rusty tractor abandoned in the grass. He panicked—he wasn't a mechanic. He threw his pack to the dirt and turned away. What if he couldn't fix it? What if he could? He imagined the great wild plain a field of grain, confined to a grid of roads and fences. A warrior screamed, and Trevor looked up to see the tractor, now a lion, with a huge mane and a flicking angry tail, coming for him, teeth bared. He turned and ran back the way he had come, but the line of warriors barred his progress. The chuff of the lion's paws sounded in the grass behind him.

Trevor lay on his back while Michael and the warriors rubbed fat and ochre into his skin.

"Too bad he's dead," Michael said. "Constance said he could help us." The other warriors keened with grief.

Trevor yelled out, "I'm not dead," but they couldn't hear him. Six warriors carried his body to the baobab tree and left him by the massive trunk, the grunt of lion and the screech of hyena nearby.

A black jackal paced on the far side of the tree, ears erect. The animal's wet tongue hung from the side of its mouth. Trevor tried to sit, to run, but he couldn't move. Tractor parts littered the grass around his body. The jackal slunk around the tree and prodded Trevor's ribs with its pointed nose. It rose on its hind legs; its body stretched and twisted grotesquely until it was no longer animal but a man with a jackal's head, its eyes lifeless golden orbs in its ebony face.

Trevor woke sweating and shaken. He staggered to the bathroom and peed, then paced around the apartment in an attempt to shake the vision of the jackal-headed man. He hunted around in his desk until he found a program he'd saved from the Cairo Museum. Leafing through the pages, he found what he was looking for—Anubis, the canid-headed god of the underworld. He read the description, then poured himself a finger of scotch. The creature was mythological, a character in a story. Not real. He had merely had a dream. He switched on the television and watched the end of a late-night movie, a comedy, and by the time he went back to bed and drifted into sleep, he was feeling much better.

But Anubis waited for him in the middle of a damp, dim cavern that smelled of mould and decomposition. Trevor huddled against the wall beneath a torch set into a sconce. The weak flame provided the only light in the place. Trevor, dressed in jeans and a black T-shirt that read *Calgary Flames*, shivered with cold and fright. Anubis fixed his glowing eyes on Trevor, who couldn't help but whimper.

"Another coward," Anubis said. He scratched his long pointed snout with the index finger of one hand, and swatted at a fly with the other. His voice was deep and dripped with disappointment. "Am'mit. Look what he's wearing. No class. What happened to the good old days when they arrived laid out and wrapped so neatly in linen?"

Am'mit shuffled out of the shadows, a tripartite hodge-podge of lion, hippo and crocodile. He drooled and licked his chops. Trevor gagged at the unbearable stench.

"Don't worry," Anubis said to Trevor. "He's more bite than his bark." Then he laughed, his muzzle raised in a haunting howl.

Anubis and Am'mit exchanged a nod, then looked up. Trevor followed their gaze.

A pure white feather dropped from the canopy of black and drifted down through slatted beams of light and shadow. The curled edges glinted as the feather twisted and turned.

It settled without a whisper on a concave dish suspended by fine gold wire. The dish dipped a hair's breadth, and Anubis let out a deep sigh. "So delicately balanced," he explained. "Nothing but the finest instruments for this weighty work."

From the surface of a stone table beside the scale, Anubis scooped up a quivering mass of flesh and cupped it in his two hands. On the other side of the balance, Am'mit belched, then gnashed his teeth. Trevor felt faint and braced himself against the icy stone wall. Anubis glanced over at him. "You foreigners don't appreciate ritual." He paused and held the contents of his hands out for Trevor. "Listen to the timeless contraction of your heart."

The crimson mound pulsed, glistening in the torchlight. The cavern filled with a rhythmic beat. Trevor covered his ears with his hands.

Anubis placed the heart carefully on the empty side of the scale. As the dish began to swing in response to the weight, he fixed Trevor with a steely stare. "Hearts don't lie," he said.

Three pairs of eyes followed the pointer as it tipped slowly back and forth across the balance mark.

"Bets Anubis?" Am'mit pleaded, rubbing his clawed paws together.

"I place no odds," Anubis scoffed. "I'm a technician, not a romantic. Either way the scale tips I will have done my job."

As the three watched, each hopeful for a different outcome, the swing of the pointer slowed. Back and forth.

Back . . . and forth.

TWENTY

❦ Trevor's Christmas dream shook him to the core. Wasn't dreaming of your own death a bad, if not fatal, sign? And worse, the dream ended before he knew what the outcome would be. At night in bed, when he closed his eyes to sleep, all he saw were the burning glow of the eyes of the man/ jackal, the pink pulsating flesh of his own leaden heart and the stinking hunger on the drooling face of Am'mit. On the Wednesday after New Year—a clear thirty-below-zero day and his fortieth birthday—he handed in his resignation. Andy read the letter and grunted. "You can pick up your cheque and a letter of reference after lunch."

The cheque was substantial, an accumulation of overtime and holiday pay plus a bonus for years of service, the letter said. He deposited it all in the bank, called the realtor's number he had noted down in the fall and drove to Millarville. The property appeared more dilapidated in the wan winter light. He parked on the road and waded through the drifts of snow down the driveway and into the yard. He dug his way through to the door with a loose board he ripped from the fence. The realtor told him he'd find the key hidden under the porch eaves. The realtor also assured him he'd get the place for a song; the owner dead three years past—suicide—and the widow desperate to sell.

The door screeched on its hinges as he stepped onto the back porch. A pair of mud-caked rubber boots was flopped over in the corner and a mildewed jacket hung stiff from a hook on the wall. He pushed open the kitchen door. A thick layer of grime caked every surface and the room reeked of rodent droppings. Trevor shivered. Except for the dirt, the room looked lived in, the table set for two, used dishes in the sink. An open tin can sat on the counter beside the stove and he blew off the dust then rolled back the curled yellowed label. *Beans with pork.* He tapped his finger on the petrified scum in the bottom of the pan and wondered if the owner had killed himself before dinner. He walked from room to room, his breath billowing out in frozen clouds of moisture. Mice scurried in the walls in response to his footsteps. In the bedroom, clothes hung in the closets, the sheets on the beds made up with hospital corners, an open jar of lotion—long dried up—on the dresser. He flipped over a dusty cushion on the couch in the living room, sat down, and picked up a *Reader's Digest* from the coffee table. *September 1981, Eat Better To Live Better.* Through the filthy picture window, the Rocky Mountains loomed, majestic, covered with snow and closer than he would have guessed. He thought about the owners in their youth, a young married couple, laying out the foundation, situating the house for the best view, innocent of the tragic end to the fairytale. They probably knew the names of all the mountain peaks on the horizon. Turning this place into a farm again would take a lot of work, but at least it would divert his mind from the ruins of his life. He could join a community group, learn square dancing, meet farmers' daughters. Or he'd turn into one of those eccentric old codgers who lived by themselves and chased intruders off with a shotgun.

"What are you doing?"

Trevor looked up, startled. Angela stood in the doorway to the kitchen. Why hadn't he heard the squeal of the door or the sound of her footsteps across the creaking linoleum?

"I should ask the same thing," he said. "Where did you come from?"

"I followed you." Her hair was up and she wore office clothes: a knee-length black parka, navy wool pants. The cuffs of her pants and her boots were coated with snow. Trevor ached at the sight of her.

"Followed me?" He struggled to form words into sentences. "Why?"

"I was on my way to your apartment and I saw you leave," she said.

"I could have been going to work," he stammered.

"No, you weren't." She eyed him. "I called your office. They said you didn't work there anymore."

"Well," he muttered, "I quit."

"That explains what you're doing in an old run-down farmhouse at thirty below."

"I'm thinking of uh . . . putting in an offer," he confessed, knowing there was no use lying to her when she was on the trail of the truth.

Angela walked across the floor. Her boots clicked on the wide scuffed planks. Snowy footsteps trailed after her. She watched his face the whole time. She sat in an overstuffed armchair across from him, oblivious to the swirl of dust around her. "This. You're buying this?"

"I'm thinking of it. As a matter of fact I'm pretty sure of it." He crossed his legs with feigned confidence. "I've had enough of the city." He wished Angela would turn off her lawyer eyes.

"By yourself?"

"What were you doing at my apartment?" He could play the cross-examination game too—he'd watched *Perry Mason* every Wednesday night with Aunt Gladys, their one shared pleasure. "In the middle of a work day. And hey, you're supposed to be in Swede Lake. I thought you took a leave."

"I have a problem legal aid client. He insists on working with me."

"What does that have to do with me?"

"Not a thing. But I thought you might be interested in this." Angela drew an envelope from her pocket and tapped it against her leg. "Who's Constance?"

"What?"

"Constance, who is she?" Angela asked again. Outside, the wind was rising. The loose shingles rattled on the roof.

"A friend." Trevor searched his memory, positive he had told Angela about Constance. "I mentioned her to you. She's that old lady I met in Frankfurt."

"I remember. But who is she?"

"A friend."

"You already said that. Why would she write me a letter?"

"Constance wrote to you?" Trevor choked at the news. He hadn't heard from the old woman since the end of September. Her phone in Sooke was cut off. "When?"

"Last week. Dated December 12."

"But how did she get your address?"

"Good question. She claimed there weren't many law firms in Calgary with a lawyer named Angela."

"Well." Trevor fumbled for words. "How is she?"

"I don't know. She talked about you."

"What did she say?"

"Oh, that she hoped I wouldn't give up on you. That you were—how did she put it—a diamond in the rough. Unlike the typical outwardly attractive, inwardly shallow male, you are like buried treasure. That is, once dusted and polished." Angela continued to tap the edge of the envelope on her leg. "She went on for quite a few pages."

"She always had this unrealist—" Trevor paused. "Constance had a lot of faith in me. I saved her life, you know."

"No, I don't. You never told me the story." Her sarcasm cut deep. "Why don't you fill me in?"

By the time Trevor told Angela the entire saga—his meeting of Constance, their adventure in Cairo, the great rescue—his hands were numb and his lips had to work to form words.

"You didn't tell her to write to me?"

"No," Trevor said, "I swear I didn't." He ran his index finger across his chest. "Cross my heart."

Angela studied him. "I gotta go. I have an appointment." She stood, the side of her coat grey with dust.

Trevor groped for the right words to make her stay. Perhaps if he could sustain the conversation about Constance, her unwavering belief in him might brush off on Angela and she'd change her mind. Trevor pointed at the envelope in her hand. "Can I read her letter?"

"Oh," she said as if she had forgotten she still held it in her hand. "I didn't bring her letter. This is for you." She held the envelope out to him. "We found your brother."

An hour later, Trevor stepped from the farmhouse into a chinook wind that blew strong and steady down from the mountains, the air now warm and earthy. Water dripped from icicles along the eaves. He slid through the melting snow to the car and kicked the slush from his boots before getting in. As he drove away, he took one more look back at the farm. He wondered if Angela had remembered today was his birthday.

TWENTY-ONE

The wipers smeared a paste of snow and frozen rain across the windshield. The cloud-burdened sky weighed on the earth like a heavy greatcoat. The wind buffeted the car from the northwest, almost blowing it from the highway at times. Trevor frowned through the gaps between the opaque ever-changing mess and hunted for the truck stop Brent described on the phone. Twenty kilometres west of Edmonton on Highway 16, near Spruce Grove. He didn't relish the notion of a night at a truck stop and prayed the highways department wouldn't close the road to Calgary before the end of the day. The thought of a reunion with his brother conjured up a mixture of trepidation and anticipation. After Aunt Gladys's funeral in Regina sixteen years ago, they were so happy to get back into their Gladys-free lives that they had eliminated one another as well. Brent had sounded pleased to hear from Trevor last week, amused that Angela's law firm had tracked him down.

"At least it wasn't the cops," he had joked over the phone.

The navy and white Husky sign loomed out of the sleet, and Trevor turned the car into the parking lot where half a dozen rigs lined the north side. Trevor wondered which of the mammoth machines belonged to Brent. His brother had loved his machines: fast cars, motorbikes, knobby wheeled trucks on high suspension. He spent most of his adolescence—when not truant from school or prowling with his buddies—out in the backyard, tinkering with one engine or another.

Trevor stepped through the door of the coffee shop, stamped the weather from his boots, and shook snowflakes and water from the shoulders of his duffle coat. The sign above his head read *All Day Breakfast*. The warm room smelled of coffee, bacon and cigarette smoke. He scanned the tables for Brent and felt the familiar search pattern click in—big brother equals safety. He wasn't prepared for the man in the grease-stained cap, plaid shirt and faded jean jacket who rose from a booth by the window and strode toward him, hand outstretched. Trevor could handle the bushy beard, the sag of pot belly over the waistband and the beefy arms, but Brent would be taller with fire in his eyes. This man looked tired and defeated, a half a head shorter than Trevor. He remembered gazing up, always up, in awe at his big brother.

"Trevor, buddy." The man grabbed Trevor and crushed him against his chest. "How the fuck you doin'?" Trevor almost choked on the smell of tobacco, unwashed hair and stale beer.

Trevor stood back and studied the man. "Brent?"

"Don't know me with the beard, eh?" Brent guffawed. "Hell, I've had this bush for thirteen years. I'd feel naked without it."

"Yeah, the beard." Trevor said lamely. "It's the beard." He clapped his brother on the shoulder. "Great to see you."

Trevor followed Brent back to the booth and ate scrambled eggs and toast while Brent drank black coffee and chain smoked. The gale outside the window blew gusts of frozen rain across the parking lot.

"Nice coat," Brent said. "You done all right for yourself."

"I've got a decent job, I guess," Trevor lied, feeling self-conscious about his clean pressed corduroy shirt with the label on the pocket and his duffle coat crumpled on the seat beside him. He wished he'd worn his jeans. "I travel a lot, which is a pain in the ass."

Brent grunted. "Me too."

Trevor studied the row of rigs in the parking lot. "Which one's yours?"

"Wine cab." Brent gestured with his hand toward a double semi parked at the edge of the lot. His fingers trembled; ash threatened to tip from his cigarette onto the table.

"Are you going to be okay in this weather?"

"This little bit of snow? It's nothin'. Don't you worry about me. I've run this friggin' route for eight years from Saskatoon through Edmonton to Vancouver. I could drive it with one arm tied behind my back. You're the one who's going to have trouble in that sissy car." He pointed his nicotine-stained finger at Trevor's hatchback parked up against the building. "Can that thing drive through air?" He laughed at his own joke and Trevor relaxed at the tease.

"You got an old lady yet?" Brent grinned, smoke lacing across his face. "You were never one for the babes."

When Angela had handed Trevor the envelope with Brent's phone number, he wondered from the expression on her face if she knew more than she let on. Has she had legal aid clients like Brent?

"I'm seeing a pretty nice lady, the one who found you for me," he fibbed again. He hadn't seen Angela since his birthday.

"Right, the lawyer. Sexy phone voice." Brent winked.

"And you?" Trevor steered the conversation away from his non-existent love life.

"Naw, I had one a couple years back. Cheryl." He stretched out her name like warm taffy, like he wanted to savour the experience. "But she walked out on me."

"Another guy?"

Brent stubbed his cigarette out in the ashtray. "Nope." He lit another. "I got this bad habit you see."

"Booze?"

"Well, two bad habits. The other one's white and real soft and makes you feel fine. Too much competition for Cheryl." Brent picked up his jean jacket. "Come see my rig."

Trevor paid the bill and followed Brent across the tarmac. The snow had eased, and they lingered outside the semi for a few minutes while Brent listed off the specs: length, weight, capacity, axles, horsepower.

"This thing must cost a pretty penny," Trevor said as they walked the perimeter of the huge machine.

Brent shook his head. "Not mine. I lease it from the company. Tried buying one a few years ago, but the bank ended up with it." He clambered like a monkey up the cab and opened the door. Trevor scrambled after him into a miniature hotel room.

"Hey," he said. "It's not so different from our clubhouse in the maple in Aunt Gladys's backyard."

"Aunt Glad-Ass, don't you mean." They both snickered. "Better. The club didn't have no TV or refrigerator and this one sure as hell ain't gonna collapse."

They laughed again. A familiar ease slipped over Trevor's shoulders like an old sweater. He settled into the passenger's seat and swivelled around to face the sleeping berth with its tousled bedclothes, a girly magazine open at the centrefold, and wondered where Brent hid his soft white other woman. The laughing had sent Brent into a fit of coughing that reminded Trevor of Uncle Pat before he died.

"Do you remember Mom?" He surprised himself with the question.

Brent wiped the spittle from his mouth with the back of his sleeve. "Course I remember Mom. Dumb question."

"I don't."

Brent leaned against the berth, crossed his arms, and studied Trevor's face. "You don't?" he said. "I guess you were a little pisser."

"Tell me about her."

Brent lifted his cap with one hand and brushed back greasy thinning hair with the other. "Well, let me see. She was one fine lady. Reminded me of the Queen. You remember those pictures of Queen Elizabeth on the wall in school. Like that. Except her hair was darker and she wore it long."

Trevor tried to conjure up a picture of his mother in his head and came up with the beautiful woman in his dream on the plane to Cairo. May.

"And she laughed a lot and did the craziest things. One time I remember we went down to the dugout to catch frogs with her. It was so hot, she jumped in, clothes and all. Then she chased after us around the dugout with her dress stuck to her. She used to make the best rhubarb pie."

"Did she . . ."

Trevor hesitated, his next question the real reason he made this journey to the greasy spoon truck stop on Highway 16 in an ice storm in the middle of winter. The question that had lurked in his mind since the day the news of his parents' accident changed his life. The opportunity to ask it had come, and he was terrified of the answer.

"Did she . . ." he repeated.

"Cough it up, for Chrissake."

"Did she like me?"

Brent slapped his leg and roared. "Like you. Like you? You're shittin' me. You were Mama's little favourite. Dad used to complain she never got anything done because you were always on her lap. I would say she liked you."

"Did you mind?" Trevor stuttered at this unexpected news. "I mean that I was the favourite."

"Hell, no. I liked you myself." Brent reached over and punched Trevor gently on the shoulder. Tears burned at the back of Trevor's eyes. He crooked his arm around his brother's neck, and knuckled Brent's scalp. Brent's cap flipped off onto the floor and he retrieved it with a grin. "Got any more dumb questions?"

Trevor had one more but knew that any grown man would scoff at the idea of a five-year-old child causing a fiery car crash from miles away. He knew a child was never a sin. That accidents happened. And hearts failed.

"No, no more dumb questions. But . . ." Trevor paused. "I'm thinking of buying a farm."

Brent's face lit up. "Yeah? Where 'bouts?"

"Millarville."

"Cattle round there?"

"I'm thinking of doing a mix. Sunflowers. Or ostrich. They say you can make a lot of money off ostrich."

"Ostrich?" Brent chortled. "I hear they can kick the shit outta you. Let me know if you do it. I'll come out and give you a hand."

"That'd be great." Trevor imagined the two of them lassoing one of the great flapping birds. "Listen, I'd better head off. I want to be home before dark. And before they close the road."

"Yeah, I need to push on too. Damn, they need their Alberta steaks in Vancouver."

Trevor hugged his brother. "Don't be a stranger."

"You can call me at the dispatch centre any time night or day."

"Give me your home number."

Brent waved his hand around the tiny cab. "Home sweet home."

They climbed down from the truck and shuffled side by side on the snow-swept pavement, hands stuffed in their pockets.

"Good, snow's stopped," Brent said. "You should be okay."

"Yeah." Trevor answered. "Well," he held out his hand, "you take care."

But Brent stepped in and hugged him. "Call me soon, kid," he said.

Trevor turned and started for his car, but he hadn't taken three steps when Brent called after him. "Trev?"

Trevor turned. Brent stood, hands in the pockets of his jeans, shirttail drifting below his jacket, looking like a hopeful dog. "I . . . I wonder if you might have a few extra bucks. I'm in a bad spot. I'll get it back to you the end of the month."

Trevor pulled out his wallet and stuffed all the bills he had—two fifties and three twenties—into his brother's hand.

"Don't worry about it," he said. "Any time."

The coyote prowled the perimeter of the farmyard. His nostrils flared at the warm wind that carried the scent of human between the buildings. The odour both attracted and repelled him. He often observed the two-legged animals from a distance, curious about their activities, yet equally cautious. Faint memories of a gentle touch on his back mingled with the revulsion of confinement. Beneath the human smell hung the aroma of prey, and the promise of easy hunting, which along with the cold had driven him in from the wind-swept plain.

Under cover of dark, he dug along the gap in the foundation of the building where he heard the lazy croon of the languid, slow-moving birds he desired. His joints ached with age and he tired easily; the winter had been hard.

His attempts to secure a mate had proven successful but more difficult. For three weeks he presented himself with the other males, but each female in turn rebuffed him in favour of the youngsters, many his own offspring. Finally, a five-year-old bitch accepted him. So far, she had responded to his attempts to mate by snapping at his nose or sitting with her tail curled between her legs.

He surrendered to the henhouse; the gaps in the boards, which had provided entry in previous forays, had been patched with wire and wood. The barn was his next target, with its promise of mice or the unwary cat, but as he skirted across the back of the yard toward the red and white building, he heard the bark of the dog and retreated into the night, stomach empty.

TWENTY-TWO

Caesar A. met Trevor's car at the road. The dog turned circles in a frenzy of excitement and wove down the driveway in the beam of the headlights. When Trevor stepped from the car in front of the house, the dog forgot his manners and jumped up, front paws on Trevor's abdomen, and tried to lick his face.

"Caesar, get off." Helen hurried down the porch steps, drying her hands on a tea towel. Caesar dropped to all fours and squirmed in tight circles around Trevor's legs. "You're a sight for sore eyes. 'Bout time," she said as she hugged him. Her hair, her blouse, smelled of fresh bread and fish. "Come in before I catch a death of cold."

Axel's face broke into a grin the moment he saw Trevor. "Thought you'd dropped off the face of the planet, son," he said, pumping Trevor's hand.

"I . . . I've been . . . busy," Trevor mumbled, thrown off kilter by their enthusiastic welcome and the insinuation he had been missed.

"Sit down, there's leftovers," Helen ordered. She ladled out an off-white mound of jelly with a side of mashed potatoes, peas and soft pale flatbread onto the plate in front of Trevor. "That's *lefsa*, potato pancake." Helen pointed at the flatbread.

"And this?" Trevor aimed his fork at the mound.

"*Lutefisk*. It's cod. A Swedish Christmas dish. We didn't have the energy to cook Christmas dinner this year, but Axel and I've been craving it so Nancy brought a package up from Lethbridge last week."

Trevor cringed at the smell of the quivering mass of cod as she poured melted butter and white sauce over it. "No pie today, but I've got canned cherries for ice cream." She turned back to the counter.

"You didn't offer me any dessert," Axel complained as he pulled up a chair across from Trevor.

Helen plunked a mug of tea in front of Axel. "You're not company. Never you mind, you can have the cherries. But no ice cream." She leaned in close to Trevor and whispered. "Doctor put him on a diet last month—hypoglycemia."

"Helen," Axel protested. "Don't go bothering Trevor with our little troubles. Might scare him away again."

Trevor looked down at the plate of steaming food in front of him and knew it wouldn't be the talk that scared him away.

"Go on," Helen urged. "I know it's not the prettiest dish in creation. Don't worry, the lye's all washed out."

"Lye?"

"It preserves the fish. Can't use my good silver with it though."

Trevor picked up his fork—he couldn't bear to disappoint them again—and slipped a mouthful of the warm fishy mush through his lips. He forced it down his throat, trying not to gag. "Good," he smiled and nodded, hoping he was being convincing. "Different."

Helen slapped her thigh. "I knew it. A Scandinavian at heart."

The second forkful went down his throat with less difficulty and as he worked his way through the pile he discovered melted butter and white sauce rendered each mouthful tolerable, particularly with a milk chaser. Almost tasty.

Helen and Axel watched over him as he ate the entire plateful. When done, he slapped his stomach with both hands for effect.

"There's more." Helen started for the stove.

"No," he said with more haste than intended. "I'd better save room for the dessert."

Helen cleared his dishes and started to wash up. "Dessert later. Tell us why you're here. Haven't seen you in months, and we know you didn't follow the smell of *lutefisk* all the way from Calgary." Helen winked at Axel.

Trevor pushed his chair back from the table. "I didn't think I was welcome here after . . . well, you know."

"Yes, we know. Angela told us a fool story about a game of shinny down in Swede Lake. That you caused Bjorne's heart attack." Helen threw the dishrag into the water and soapsuds splashed onto the floor. "Pile of nonsense. He did himself in, the damn idiot. Wouldn't quit smoking. Besides," she turned and scrutinized him, "whose idea was that game?"

Trevor shrugged. "We were both pretty drunk."

"You can't fool me." She pointed her finger at him. "I know it was Bjorne's idea—kind of stupid thing he'd do. You got more sense. The fool dug his own grave."

"Doesn't matter anyhow," Axel said. "What's done is done. Important thing is Trevor's here."

"Why are you here if you didn't think you were welcome?" Helen put her soapy hands on her hips. "I hope it's cause you worked up the courage to face up to Angie. She blows on you once and you're flat on your back."

"I . . . I had hoped I'd find Angela here," Trevor stuttered, not sure if standing up to Angela or lying down with her was what he wished to accomplish.

"She wouldn't let you in the door anyhow," Helen said. "She's up at Bjorne's house. Got back from Calgary an hour ago from one of her hopeless cases that can't do without her. That hasn't changed. She drags home the sorriest strays you ever saw. We had cats, dogs, mice—you name it. Bull snake, barn owl. Remember the cayoot, Axel?"

Axel bobbed his head in his slow methodical way. "Carlos. Rescued it from a hawk; that animal followed her everywhere. Angela was about thirteen when he hit cayoot puberty. One tail-flick from a pretty female and he took off."

"Broke her heart," Helen said. "She swore she saw him

down at the cabin a few times but the mangy creature wouldn't let her near him."

"We saw one in October after the funeral," Trevor remembered. "Old guy, torn ear I think."

"Torn ear, eh?" Axel's tufted eyebrows, big and feathery as moths, twitched at the information. "Couldn't be. Cayoots rarely live that long. Maybe one of his pups, like Caesar A."

"Carlos was Caesar's dad?"

"Might be. A male got to our collie bitch ten years ago and we figured it was Carlos. The others are too shy to come so close to the farm."

"That animal you saw better leave my chickens alone or he'll join his ancestors. Something was out there last night, Axel," Helen insisted, then turned to Trevor. "When Angie lost interest in stray animals, she started bringing home stray men."

"What do you mean?"

Helen sighed. "Get the album, Axel."

"First I'll show you Carlos." Helen flipped through a few pages to find the photos of tomboy Angela with the coyote pup. "Amazing he lived. That hawk had hurt him pretty bad. She sat up with him all night for a week. You could say he was a success story. But these . . . " She opened the album to the photo of the cowboy wrapped around Angela. She couldn't have been more than seventeen.

"Blackie." Helen pointed at the cowboy.

"Blackie?"

"His name," Helen explained. "Angie found him at the fall rodeo in Brooks. Terrible drinker."

She turned the page. "And this one. Larry." Long-haired Larry wore a leather vest and bell-bottom pants. "Played in a band that went through Brooks."

"I chased him out of here the day I found marijuana plants in the back of the garden," Axel added. "Fool didn't even try to hide them."

Six more men followed, all with stories worse than the last. "The fellows she hankered after were sorrier types than the animals." Helen explained. "The ones with the sad dog faces like they'd been kicked around most of their life. She thought she could fix 'em. Like all her animals. She got bit more than a few times, though."

"Hal." Helen jabbed the photo of a man on a motorcycle with her finger.

Axel nodded. "Seemed like a nice kid at first. Came from a farm up north by Westlock. Worked at the gas station in Swede Lake."

"Nice kid? Huh. A stinking skunk," Helen snorted. "When Angie came home with bruises I wanted to go after him with a shotgun except she announced she was giving up on men. He was the last one. She started law school the next year."

Helen sighed and flipped a few pages to the final picture. Trevor, face shiny with sweat, hoisted a hay bale up onto the stack in the back of the truck. Angela watched from the forklift.

He swivelled his head from Helen to Axel and back again. "Was I . . ." he stuttered, "was I one of her strays?"

"Don't think that," Axel said.

"Don't go smoothing things over, Axel." Helen cut him short. Axel grunted, shuffled over to his chair and picked up the newspaper.

"We worried when you came out to hay. You gotta admit you look like a bit of a sad puppy. Understandable. Angie told us about your family. We thought you were another one of her projects."

"And?" Trevor asked.

Axel lifted the paper higher to hide his face. "We figured you could be fixed," Helen said.

The wind rattled down the stovepipe. "We hoped it would work out," Axel added softly from behind the paper.

"Me too," Trevor lamented. "Do you think she's seeing anyone else?"

"Not that I know of," Helen answered. "She's not the most talkative creature. But she's only left the farm for work a few times since the funeral. Or at least she tells us it's for work."

Trevor thought about their encounter at the Millarville farmhouse and cringed, remembering how cold it was, the house, her shoulder. "What about the farm?" Trevor said. "Are you selling?"

"That's Angie and Matt's idea," Helen answered. "Matt's, I think. Angie loves this farm. I can't figure her out sometimes. Axel and I aren't going anywhere."

"'Less that big-shot fella gets his way," Axel interjected from behind the paper.

"Big shot?"

"That farm corporation fella. Made us an offer last month."

"He can put it you know where." Helen crossed her arms over her bosom. "Angie thinks it's a good idea. That we'd love some retirement place in Calgary. Typical, trying to fix everybody up."

She disappeared into the pantry and returned with a jar of canned cherries and a plastic tub of ice cream. She handed Trevor the jar to open. "What do you think? Should we sell?"

Trevor struggled with the lid. "I don't know." He breathed through the effort and the ring turned loose. "No," he decided as he pried the sealer cap off with the edge of a knife. The seal sucked open and the sweet aroma of sugar-soaked cherries hit his nostrils. "But can you manage?"

"Neighbours . . . hired hand . . . you? Seeding starts in a few weeks. We could use the help." Helen passed him a mound of ice cream and a spoon. The thick syrup stained the vanilla balls crimson as he spilled the plump fruit into his bowl.

"Me?" he said as summer filled his mouth along with the cherries. "What about Angela? She won't talk to me."

"A girl likes to be pursued." Helen tilted her head at her husband. "Right, Axel?"

Axel lowered the paper below the tops of his reading glasses. "I walked ten miles, uphills both ways, in snow, hail, tornadoes, every Sunday to court Helen. I think she let me in the door after a year. Let me kiss her after the second. Married the third."

It was the longest speech Trevor had ever heard from the man.

"Listen to him," Helen interrupted. "Spare us."

Trevor stirred the ice cream into a pink soup. He looked hopefully up at the two. "What should I do?"

"One minute." Helen vanished into the pantry again. The two men listened to the slide of drawers, the clatter of utensils, and miscellaneous rustles and clunks from the tiny room. The grandfather clock bonged nine times. A cat sauntered in from the bedroom and lapped at her dish. Helen emerged five minutes later with a brown paper bag and plopped it down in front of Trevor.

"Peanut butter and cheese sandwiches," she declared.

"Pardon?"

"You heard what I said. Angela's favourite if you don't know, which you should," Helen snapped.

"What difference will a sandwich make?"

"You got to eat it in front of her. And act like you enjoy it. Like you did tonight with the *lutefisk*."

Trevor grinned sheepishly, then frowned. "But I don't get it," he said, his level of anxiety escalating.

"Since the age of five, she insisted any man that loved peanut butter and cheese sandwiches was for her." Helen handed him his coat. "Go on."

"She likes 'em fresh," Axel offered from behind the paper.

Trevor stepped out onto the driveway and buttoned up his coat. The temperature had dropped and the wind had risen. The cold stung his bare cheeks as he trudged toward Bjorne's house. His feet crunched in the dry packed snow. Above, clouds scudded across the night sky and stars gleamed through the intermittent gaps in the cloud cover. He tucked the paper bag with the sandwich inside his coat and shoved his hands into his pockets for warmth. He rounded the corner of the barn in time to see Angela climb into the cab of Bjorne's truck and drive away down the unplowed track through the fields.

As the four-wheel drive pickup disappeared, tail lights shining, Trevor wondered where Angela was going at this time of night, but also found himself at a turning point. Since the death of his parents, he had blown through life on the winds of circumstance and the initiatives of others. His abduction to Regina, his move to Calgary, and now, a shove out the door into the cold by a Swedish farmwife.

As a lopsided moon, three days short of full, rose from the snowdrifts into the winter sky, his toes hurt, his ears burned and swirls of snowflakes settled on his hair and shoulders. Ahead, down an uncertain road, drove the woman he loved. At his back, Calgary and the Millarville farm, a fresh start. Alone. By tomorrow the sandwich would turn stale and dry, like his prospects with Angela. Hadn't Helen told him Angela would turn him away? How could he convince her of his intentions, his potential for fixing . . . no, not that, his solid character and undying love. He recalled Helen's uncertainty about Angela's trips to Calgary. Was there another man in the truck with her? He should return to his car, to Calgary. Trevor swivelled, boots squeaking in the new snow. "No, Trevor. Take chances," the voice of Constance whispered in his left ear. "A girl likes to be pursued," Helen said in his right.

Two foolish old women. They meant well, but how could he barge into Angela's life and demand to be heard. She'd hate him for sure. She knew where to find him if she wanted him. He pushed the voices in his head away, but they persisted. "Take chances." "Pursue her." "Take chances."

"What the hell," he said out loud and made a choice . . . to take a chance, follow the taillights into the night and hope for the best.

TWENTY-THREE

❦ At the first gate, the tires of his car began to spin in the bumper deep snow and by the second the car was hopelessly stuck. He tried digging the tires free with the snow shovel he kept in the trunk, but after ten minutes he was sweating and making little progress and abandoned the effort. Ahead, illuminated by his headlights, the tracks of the truck cut a deep swath across the otherwise pristine landscape. By now, he was certain they led to the cabin. No more than a fifteen-minute walk. He warmed his cramped fingers over the heater vent, then slipped on his driving gloves, pocketed a flashlight from the cubby and turned off the ignition. After some debate, he stuffed the sandwich bag inside the front of his coat and started, on foot, down the track.

The walk proved more difficult than Trevor had anticipated. The narrow beam from the flashlight illuminated his passage a mere four steps ahead, and his boots slid in the loose snow at the bottom of the ruts, making progress slow. The gusting wind threatened to cover the trail with drifts. In a few places he waded through powder to his knees. The cold seeped in through his inadequate clothing and he knew he must keep moving.

Trevor was mulling over what he would say to Angela when he tripped, and toppled, flat on his back, into packed snow. As he fell, he noticed a flicker of movement to his left and rolled onto his shoulder to aim a beam of light into the night. A pair of amber eyes glowed from the shadows.

"Caesar?" he called, but he knew he had stepped over the sleeping dog to get out through the porch door.

The animal stepped into the diffuse light at the edge of the flashlight's reach. A coyote. It sat down on its haunches in the snow, head cocked, ears tilted forward and stared at Trevor. The velvet of the animal's left ear was ragged. Was it the coyote from the coulee last summer? Angela's Carlos? Would a coyote, an old, smart coyote, attack a grown man? Bjorne had shared a story about a newborn calf taken down by a pack of the animals; its face chewed half off, one leg torn free. Trevor's situation didn't look good. He was sprawled in the snow in the middle of the night, a flashlight for protection, a wild beast one bound away. Snow whipped into Trevor's face. He closed his eyes to the sting. What would get him first, the cold or the coyote?

When he opened his eyes, the coyote hadn't moved. Trevor eased himself to his feet, while estimating the relative distance to car or cabin. At least the cabin contained Angela and likely a warm fire. He stepped cautiously back into the ruts, and the coyote stood, bushing out its tail, now held stiffly out behind its body. Trevor took another few cautious steps forward. The animal followed, eyes fixed on Trevor's face. A blast of wind cut through Trevor's coat. He stumbled and caught himself before he fell into the deep snow again. He looked back over his shoulder. The coyote padded up beside him not two steps away. Trevor broke into a run, heart thudding, his ears filled with drumming; the coyote picked up its pace. The wind thrust against Trevor's body, and snatched his breath away, carrying it into the moaning night. After ten steps his foot slipped and he tipped forward into another snowbank. The coyote sat and watched while Trevor struggled out of the drift.

"Piss off," Trevor yelled as he whacked the snow from his coat, but the coyote only scratched its side with a hind leg, an action which Trevor found strangely reassuring. The animal appeared curious rather than aggressive. At least it wasn't growling and nipping at his heels. Maybe the creature was hungry. He dug inside his coat for the paper bag and retrieved half a sandwich. Breaking off a chunk, he tossed it in the direction of the coyote. The bread sank halfway into the snow. The animal stepped cautiously forward and pawed at the bit of sandwich. He sniffed at it, picked it up in his teeth, and backed away before swallowing it down in one gulp. Trevor tossed a second piece and a third until the half sandwich was gone, each chunk devoured with apparent enthusiasm.

"Well, that's a surprise," Trevor said. "A lover of strange concoctions. A guy for Angela." He breathed deeply, rolled his shoulder to ease the tension in his neck and resumed his trek forward. The coyote led a stride ahead and still to the left, eerily silent as it faded in and out of the arc of light.

"Carlos." Trevor said, his shoulders hunched against the cold. "That your name? Everybody thinks you're dead."

The coyote panted clouds of fog into the air as it padded through the snow.

"You one of Angela's rescues?" he continued, his words floating outward in their own vaporous balloons. "Well, me too. There's quite a club of us."

Minutes later the wind dropped without warning. The clouds parted around the moon, which hung like a shiny bent saucer above man and canine as they made their way across the blanketed earth. Reflected moonlight bathed the pair in a gentle luminescence. Trevor turned off the flashlight and gazed skyward at the display.

"There's Orion," he explained to Carlos, who walked on without heed. "And the Dippers. Now where's the dog?" He spun in place. "Can't find it. The moon's too bright. You know, Carlos, according to my friend Constance, you're a moon in orbit. Split off from the mother planet, which would be Angela. You're her—" Trevor lowered his eyes from the heavenly array to Carlos, who was now lying on his stomach in the rut a few steps ahead of Trevor, licking his paws, "her coyote moon," he whispered, "which would make me . . ." His frigid brain churned to form the next logical thought in the progression. "Would make me her . . ."

But his attention was drawn ahead where a distant light glowed warm on the other side of the dark night.

"The cabin," he shouted and punched the air with his flashlight. "We're there, Carlos, we're there."

TWENTY-FOUR

When Trevor passed the truck and started down the coulee bank, the coyote slipped into the night, the tip of its tail the last glimpse of the animal Trevor would see. Across the ravine, smoke eddied down from the chimney with the rise of a fresh wind; the scent of burning logs promised a warm dry refuge. He struggled up the embankment and onto the porch, hesitating in front of the door. What if she wasn't alone? His stomach twisted at the thought, and he looked back into the dark, freezing, coyote-filled night. His fingers ached and the big toe on his left foot was numb. Before he could knock, the door swung inward and Angela stepped into the doorway. A rectangle of lamplight spilled out from behind her.

"Trevor?" she stammered.

"Hi," he answered, digging his hands into his pockets.

"What in God's name are you doing here? I heard footsteps." She wore a parka over her slacks and a sweater. Trevor's stomach untwisted one turn at the knowledge she wasn't in bed with someone else.

"I stopped at your parents'. They said you were at Bjorne's. I saw the tracks so . . . Can we talk?"

"No." She glanced behind her. "It's . . . not a good time."

The knot retied. Take chances. Take chances. "It can't wait," he said.

She scowled; light glittered on the snowflakes in her loose hair. "I said no." She rubbed her hands on her arms. "Go back to Mom and Dad's. It's freezing out here. Where's your car?"

"Stuck in a drift about halfway back. I'm not leaving." Trevor insisted. "Besides, there's a coyote out there."

"Where?" Angela peered around him into the night. "It won't hurt you. You walked here?"

"I want to talk."

"Good grief." Angela sighed and stepped back. "Get in here before you catch pneumonia."

Trevor walked into the room, which was no more than a few degrees warmer than the deep freeze outside. But the stove firebox was open and kindling crackled inside with the promise of future warmth. Angela pushed past him, tossed two split logs into the flames and clanged the cast' iron door shut. She pushed an aluminum teapot and a saucepan across the stovetop to the heat before turning to him.

"Well?" she said, crossing her arms.

His eyes scanned the room. A hiking pack was propped against the wall, boxes and tins jumbled across the plank shelf, and the end of a sleeping bag hung down over the edge of the loft. Angela's characteristic mess—the table silted over with books and papers, clothes littering the floor—was older, days older, than an hour. And she was alone.

"What's going on?" he asked.

"That's my question." The pot began to sizzle and Angela stirred its contents with a wooden spoon. "What are you doing here?"

Now that he was in her presence with the opportunity to plead his case, Trevor's brain had seized up and words failed him.

"Well?"

"I . . . I need to explain to you about the Trevor-shaped space," he blurted out, "and the moon and how the moon belongs in the—"

"What the hell are you talking about?" She faced him, the wooden spoon in her hand, gravy dripping onto the floor.

"Carlos," he mumbled. Water splashed onto his sock and he looked down to discover snow was melting from the hem of his coat.

"Carlos? The coyote? How do you know about him?"

"He's out there." Trevor pointed through the window. "He followed me."

"Are you hypothermic?"

"He likes sandwiches. I fed him this . . ." He unzipped his coat and the paper bag fell to the floor. "It's for you. Your favourite. Mine too." He stooped and ripped open the bag, holding what was left of the sandwich out to her. "Peanut butter and cheese."

Her head jerked up in surprise. "Who have you been talking—"

"I . . . I love you, Ang." His voice faded along with his resolve.

Angela's face flushed crimson, but underneath the colour her cheeks were pale in the muted cast of the kerosene lantern on the table, creases he hadn't noticed before punctuated the corners of her mouth, making her look almost old. Trevor wanted to kiss them away. "Don't call me Ang," she whispered. "That belonged to Bjorne."

"Angela, I . . ."

What would Constance do in a situation like this? She'd have Angela sharing her life story over tea in fifteen minutes. Her strange power over people. But he wasn't Constance. Not even close.

"I told you I didn't want to see you," Angela snapped. "And in case you haven't got the picture," she waved the wooden spoon around the room, "I came here to be alone."

"Your parents told me you were staying at Bjorne's."

"I . . . I couldn't stand to be there." She whirled from him and strode over to the west window where icy flakes pattered like flung grains of sand against the pane. The old glass distorted her reflection. "Please go."

Trevor's outstretched hand dropped in defeat to his hip. He'd tried, taken the chance and lost. The possibility of Angela and an uncertain but long future with her gone. He stepped forward, placed the sandwich gently on the table and zipped up his coat. When he swung open the door, a blast of frigid air and snow blew in around him, enveloping him in a chill of sadness. "If I don't make it back to the car," he yelled over the storm, "bury me in Swede Lake. Near Bjorne." Before he stepped out into the blizzard, he spun around to address her back. "And Angela. It wasn't my fault."

By the time Trevor slid to the bottom of the coulee and up the other side, and waded through the drifts to the truck, both he and his flashlight showed signs of exhaustion. The dim beam, almost useless, illuminated a small oval of twirling snowflakes. The track back to the farm was now completely obscured by drifting snow.

"Meddling old women," he growled. "Why did I ever listen to them?"

He leaned on the hood of the truck to catch his breath. A coyote howled from the other side of the vehicle, the desolate cry so close Trevor flinched. The answering call, a pitch lower, came from behind him and he twisted around and aimed his flashlight into the chaos; but the light dimmed and faltered, then blinked out. When a third howl floated over the wind from the direction of the farm, he fumbled with the truck door, clambered in and slammed down the lock with his fist.

The cab was no warmer, but he was thankful to be out of the wind and, he hoped, safe from coyotes. But not from the winter night, the numbing cold. How long could he last in here? He'd heard you go to sleep and that's that. The wails of the animals escalated—two, three, four of them; he wasn't sure. He rolled the window down a crack and tried to count them, but it was impossible. The song continually shifted and changed, one animal never sounding the same note as another.

The eerie music floated in through the space and seeped into Trevor's frozen bones. He hunched down in the seat, closed his eyes and drifted with the sounds.

The old male met his mate at the northwest edge of the coulee. Tonight she crawled in welcome on her belly and wriggled back and forth under his nose. She licked at his muzzle and nudged him with her hip as she turned. He sniffed at her tail and when, instead of snapping, she presented herself, he mounted her from behind until they were tied, then lifted his hind leg over her back to stand tail to tail. For twenty minutes, the pair remained locked together, then the conjugal tie released and they separated.

The two ran side by side along the top of the ravine, listening for mice under the crust. Tonight the rodents were plentiful and each plunge into the snow was rewarded with a squirming mouthful. The male sat, raised his slender nose to the sky, and sent out a lyrical howl. The female listened, then responded, a pitch lower. When he dropped his tone down to meet hers, she instantly climbed the scale to a falsetto. The pair breathed a duet into the night, up an octave, down. An ancient announcement to the world.

"Trevor!" He woke startled, thinking the animals were calling out his name. Maybe hypothermia had struck, or the dog-headed Egyptian God Anubis had come to guide him into death. He cleared the condensation and an edge of frost from the window, his arm sluggish and heavy, and pressed his eyes against the ice-etched glass. All he could see was blowing snow. Then out of the maelstrom, a vision emerged—hair flying out behind, eyes wild, coat open. "Trevor!" Angela screamed his name as she ran through the night.

The heat of the stew filtered from Trevor's stomach through his limbs. The woodstove pumped warmth into the room against the gaps between the logs of the walls where snow blew through in tiny white clouds.

"It's good," he said.

"It's canned." Angela leaned on her elbows across the table and watched Trevor eat. "I'm sorry," she said. "That was stupid of me to let you go back out there. No person in their right mind should be outside tonight."

He paused, a spoonful halfway to his mouth. "Gee, thanks."

"No, I didn't mean . . ." She sat up. Irritation flashed across her face. "Never mind." She stood and walked to the stove to add another log, then paced a line between the west window and the table. "Those coyotes were sure weird, so near the truck," she added. Trevor finished the soup, all the while watching her nervous striding.

"Am I like Carlos to you?" he asked finally.

"What?" She stopped her metronome of motion and studied him, then fought a grin. "Maybe the thick fur and four legs, but not the beady eyes."

He laughed for what felt like the first time in days. "No, I mean . . ."

She sat and stared at the floor. "I know what you mean."

"Helen showed me—"

"The mug shots?"

He nodded.

She absently flipped open the cover of a book on the table with a finger, closed it and opened it again. "I have clients with stories as bad as yours."

"Really?"

"One whose story isn't so different."

"What do you mean?"

"Parents lost young, no grandparents, tough childhood,"

she said, looking him in the eye. "He robs banks and kills people. You can't trust him."

"You don't trust me?" Trevor asked.

Angela didn't answer.

"Tell me then." Trevor leaned his chair back so it balanced on two legs, and flipped his spoon between his fingers. "Why aren't I a psychotic bank robber killer?"

"Luck?" she answered. "Or your awful uncle and aunt who rescued you from the ten foster homes by fifteen. And a brother who loves you."

Trevor's chair thumped upright and the spoon dropped to the table. Uncle Pat and Aunt Gladys as saviours?

"I know it wasn't your fault." She shifted her gaze from him to the table.

"Pardon?" He was still back with his new, kinder, aunt and uncle.

"Bo's heart attack." She slid her hand across the table and took his fingers in hers. "I know it wasn't your fault. Mom and I had a big fight about it before Christmas. That's when I moved over to Bo's. But I knew she was right."

"Then why wouldn't you see me?" he asked, intent on the heat that eased from her fingertips into his.

"I'm a Steffansson. Mules every one." She released his fingers and dropped her hands into her lap. "And some dumb idea I had that if you don't get close to people, you don't have to worry about losing them . . . or getting hurt."

The words clicked into place like a round peg in a round hole. "Yeah," he said lamely. "Sounds familiar. The problem is . . ." The pop and crackle of burning wood filled the space left by his unfinished sentence.

"The problem is . . . ?"

"The problem is . . . according to Constance, you've got a Trevor-shaped hole and a matching moon in orbit you can never get rid of."

She raised her eyebrows. "You and Constance had quite the conversations." She laughed. "I think you need some sleep. Let's go to bed."

"Sleep, right." He stood and steadied himself on the back of the chair, limbs like limp pasta. "Where would you like me? I could crash on the bench if you give me a blanket or a couple of jackets."

"No." She tilted her head toward the loft. "Up there with me."

"In your bed?"

She smiled. "According to Constance, sounds like I'm stuck with you."

While Angela stoked and dampered the stove down for the night, Trevor climbed the ladder to the loft with a lantern and shed his clothes, folding them into a neat pile which he deposited against the wall. Clothes, magazines and an assortment of plates and mugs littered the cramped space. He had to pick his way on hands and knees to the mattress. He unzipped the sleeping bag and shook it open. Crumbs cascaded onto the mattress, and as he brushed them off he felt a pair of eyes watching. He turned, startled, to see a photo of Bjorne propped in the corner. Trevor stopped brushing at the sight of his friend.

"I suppose I'll have to get used to it," he said to Bjorne. He stretched out on the mattress and pulled the bag up over him, the crumbs bearable if he lay still.

"Want some dessert?" Angela's head appeared at the top of the ladder and she set a plate on the edge of the loft while she scrambled up the last two rungs. Plate in hand, she crawled onto the mattress, then held it out to Trevor. The remaining half of the peanut butter and cheese sandwich. "Here, I brought your favourite."

He chuckled. "I was just—"Angela's face was deadpan, "—thinking about that sandwich. Wondering what happened to it. You read my mind."

He propped his shoulders against the pillow, picked up the sandwich and took a bite. Angela scrutinized him as he chewed. He was tempted to give her a pen and paper to take notes, but he was too tired even to choke on the dry bread and thick, gummy interior.

"Don't you want a bite?" he mumbled, peanut butter pasted to the roof of his mouth.

"No, I'm not hungry," she teased. "But let's save it. We can bury it with you in the Swede Lake cemetery."

Angela undressed and burrowed under the covers beside him. She traced circles around his navel with her fingertips. His body twitched in response. "Good, isn't it?" she sighed.

He swallowed the last gooey mouthful. "Mmmhmm." The plate dropped to the floor as he spooned into her body, a breast cupped in his hand. "Excellent."

"I mean the sandwich."

"That too."

Trevor soaked in the warmth of Angela's body. Outside the wind howled like a whole pack of coyotes. "The cheese cuts the heaviness of the peanut butter, doesn't it?" he whispered into her neck. But Angela didn't answer; she was already asleep.

TWENTY-FIVE

W "Mr. Wallace? Mr. Trevor Wallace." The woman in the doorway of his apartment scanned him up and down.

"Yes?" he answered, propping the door open with his foot, arms full of bed linens.

"But you're so young," she said in a hushed voice.

Trevor stepped back in surprise, not because the woman appeared astonished at his age—she was not much older than he —but because she was a younger version of an old friend. The same intense eyes, the diminutive stature, the shape of the face, the aura of kind assurance. Constance from forty years ago, without the cotton candy wig, the apple-doll face and the quiver in her hands. This woman was . . . pretty. Her smooth, manicured fingers clutched an all too familiar bag: the canvas bag covered in bright embroidered sunflowers.

"Please, excuse me." The woman extended her hand. "I'm Susan Arnold. I believe you knew my mother, Constance Ebenezer."

"Constance?" Trevor continued to stare at the bag, which he noticed was more worn and faced since he'd last seen it. "Yes . . . I knew her."

"Would you mind if I came in for a few moments?" she asked.

"Oh, sure." Trevor shifted to let her pass. "Come in. Sorry about the mess. I'm moving."

The apartment was in a state of uncharacteristic chaos: half full packing boxes in awkward places throughout the living room, dishes wrapped in newsprint on the table. He dropped his armload on the kitchen table, then cleared a stack of towels to make room for her on the couch. Through the picture window, the Bow River, swollen with spring runoff, rushed past.

"Can I offer you a drink? Tea? Coffee?" Trevor said, not sure if he had ever had tea in his house. He'd run out of fresh coffee beans yesterday.

"No thank you. I hope this won't take long."

"How is Constance?" Trevor said. "I haven't heard from her in a few months. I suppose you know you look like her."

The woman pulled a tissue from her pocket and dabbed at the corners of her eyes. "Mr. Wallace. My mother died four months ago—on Christmas Day."

"Oh." Trevor managed only the single word. When his parents died, the news had overwhelmed him like the twister that roared through the farm one summer and sucked up everything that lay around unsecured: soil and branches, toys and tools. The wind had sucked everything out of him too, until he could no longer feel. Bjorne's death gripped his heart like a vice. But this news hit him like an enormous powder puff, drifts of rose-scented talcum spilling over his face and down his neck. "Oh," he repeated. "I'm . . . sorry."

Waves of emotion—pain, suspicion, reluctance—washed across the woman's face one by one, then settled into a smooth picture of self-control. "I'll get right to the point. My mother . . . she . . . well, she had a strange request in her will," she said. "She asked us—my brothers and me—to give her ashes to you."

Trevor blinked. "She did?"

"Yes, and she wanted us to give you this letter." Susan drew an envelope from the flowered bag and held it out to him. "None of us have read it. But I have to tell you my brothers and I have discussed this at length. Whether to carry out her wishes. We had never heard of you. And well, my mother behaved irrationally for several years. We rarely saw her. She disappeared for close to a year. My brothers and I were worried sick. We had the police searching . . . it turns out she took herself travelling, alone, all over the world."

"Yes, I know," Trevor said.

Susan opened her mouth to speak, then closed it again. She settled the sunflower bag on the floor and cleared her throat. "Mr. Wallace. Were you and my . . ." A flush of red spread across her cheeks. "What was the nature of your relationship with my mother?"

Trevor took a moment to comprehend the implications of Susan's question. Memories of Constance played through his mind: her chatter, her flirtations, her ascension of the pyramid, clothes flapping in the wind. Her delicate fingers as she opened the lids of her boys. He laughed. Susan half stood as if ready to run for the door.

"I . . . we . . . you think your mother and I were lovers?" he blurted out.

"We had no idea who you were," she protested. "And she willed you her ashes. What were we to think?" She pursed her lips and fiddled with the handle of the flowered bag.

"I suppose that makes sense." Susan's intense scrutiny made sense of her shock at the discovery he was decades younger than her mother. "Don't worry. I knew your mother for a couple of days. We were stranded together in Cairo."

"That's it? A couple of days in Cairo, and she leaves you her ashes?" Susan raised her eyebrows in obvious disbelief.

"That's it. And the letters. She wrote me letters. I guess she took a liking to me."

"Letters?"

"Yes, I'll get them. You can read them if you want." Trevor retrieved the bundle from the desk drawer and passed the sixteen letters to Susan, who stared at the package reluctantly before she took them onto her lap. "They're all in order," he explained. She hesitated again, looked up at him, and then down at the pile before she removed the rubber band. She opened the first envelope and began to read.

Trevor resumed packing, one ear tuned for sounds from the

couch. But other than the rustle of paper as she turned pages, Susan read silently, head bowed. Trevor set aside items he wouldn't need on the farm. He pondered his weights in the back of the closet and put them in the To Sell pile, expecting he wouldn't suffer from a lack of exercise without them. He and Angela had bought Bjorne's house from Nancy; Angela convinced him the cabin could be their summer retreat or— with a mischievous smile—a playhouse for the kids. He had accepted the suggestion like he had all the others in the past two months, with a new but unexpected easy-going humour.

After half an hour he carried a glass of water to the side table, but Susan read on without a pause. He was in the bedroom folding underwear into his suitcase when he heard a sigh too big for the petite woman.

"I had no idea," she said.

Trevor returned to the living room and sat down across from her. Susan dabbed at her face with a fresh tissue, the letters scattered across the cushions.

"We would have stopped her," she said. "And father was an ogre."

Trevor covered Susan's hand with his. "She was an amazing woman," he said.

"Yes, she was." She sniffled. "Did you know she had cancer, Mr. Wallace, uterine cancer?"

Trevor shook his head. "No, is that what she died of?"

"Yes. She was diagnosed and treated a few months before she disappeared."

Trevor straightened. Before she disappeared? That meant . . . "She never told me that," he said softly.

Susan returned the letters to their envelopes, resorted them by date and set them in the middle of the coffee table in a neat pile when she was done. "I want to be honest with you. My brothers and I decided I would come here to find out who you were and what mother's connection to you was before we gave you her ashes. Frankly, if you were a lover, we decided to challenge the will for them. But . . . after reading these letters . . ." She reached her younger hand into the valise, as he had watched Constance do a dozen times, and pulled out a nondescript cardboard box. "Well . . . we, I want you to have them."

"No, no." He raised his hands, palms open. "You keep them. You're her daughter."

She placed the box in his lap. "It's what she wanted. You're her friend."

December 21, 1985

My dear Trevor:

Because you are reading this letter you know I have departed on the greatest adventure yet. One which lacks a travel guide, and my most expensive trip; it cost me all my life savings. I can't give you specific directions, but one day, I'm sure we'll trip over one another again.

I apologize for keeping my cancer a secret from you. I didn't want you to feel sorry for me, or worry or stop me. My illness made me willing to take chances. I followed in a man's footsteps for most of my life. Can you imagine my sense of freedom knowing I could make my own way in the world? And I knew that the consequences of my freedom, any trouble I might get myself into, was minor compared to the journey I would take and have taken. I want you to know, Trevor, even though I didn't make it to the top of the pyramid, I have died happy. You helped me to that place. And I admit, I appreciated having a man there for a while, to get me jump-started. Thank you.

You must wonder why I have made this last

request of you. I have two reasons. You allowed me to share my travels with another human being, for three amazing days and after, through my letters. That meant a lot to me. I know you thought me a foolish old woman, but you never said it and I love you for that. Second, I know my children, bless their hearts, love me, but they would never accept or carry out the task I ask of you. I know you won't let me down. You're a fine man under your flimsy armour.

Enclosed with this letter you'll find directions for the scattering of my ashes and money to pay the expenses. When you get there, I'm sure you will know why I chose this place. I heard about it from a neighbour here in Sooke, a retired fisherman.

He told me it's a place where anything is possible.

Love,

Constance

P.S. Take good care of that nice Angela, will you dear?

VANCOUVER ISLAND
Summer 1989

Ⅲ Trevor shivered in spite of the warm August sun and the layers of signal red nylon and neoprene that covered him from head to toe. At the end of the wooden dock, an inflatable boat bobbed up and down on its mooring lines. The captain, whose name was Baxter, flipped switches and turned knobs at the console while the marine radio blared out the weather forecast for the next twenty-four hours.

"Ready?" Baxter turned to Trevor. The reflection in the man's mirror-coated sunglasses made Trevor's stomach roll.

Trevor inhaled. He had never in his life set foot on a boat. He preferred planes and had happily forked out the hundred and twenty-five dollars for the twenty-minute flight between Vancouver and Vancouver Island in order to avoid the ferry trip across the Strait of Georgia. He was a prairie boy. Boats were unnatural. This one, at no more than six metres long, was immoral.

"Are you sure it's safe?" Trevor asked.

The captain, who wore a signal red survival suit identical to Trevor's, didn't say a word, just raised his eyebrows and gestured to the calm surface of the bay with an upturned hand to underscore the obvious. The mirror of water reflected the trawlers tied to the wharf, and the rocky shore that rimmed Ucluelet Harbour. It was not yet six AM. A bevy of sport fishing boats, most smaller than Baxter's commercial whale watcher, had already headed out of the protected bay to the open ocean.

He held out his hand to Trevor. "You do want to go, don't you? Couldn't have a better day. It'll be quiet on the bank," he said.

Trevor eyed the padded bench seats designed for twenty or more tourists, the long air-filled pontoons, the twin hundred horsepower outboards idling at the stern. He jiggled the bag in his hand, feeling the weight of the plastic vitamin bottle. The way Constance wanted it. Angela and Helen had convinced him: Constance had waited on the bookshelf in the living room far too long. Three and a half years. He had intended to fulfill her wishes earlier, but something seemed always to get in the way. Seeding, irrigation, harvest. There was machinery to repair, animals to tend to. The wedding, which took place down by the coulee. And of course, the birth of little Bo, now two. It was time to set her free. What had the old woman said about trusting in the universe? He tipped his head back to face the flawless sky and sent a request to whatever or whoever might receive it. Baxter's firm grip guided him into the boat.

Trevor took the centre seat—the centre of the centre seat—and clutched the bag of ashes close to his body. Baxter piloted the inflatable through the tight confines of the harbour and the narrow entrance marked by channel buoys, and out into open water. Baxter was right. The water was as flat as glass; not even a gentle swell nudged the shore. The boat cut through the silvery surface. Waves hissed from the bow in two equal halves; a frothy wake bubbled behind.

Trevor fixed his gaze straight ahead, toward Japan, the sun warm against his back. Eight kilometres. That was what Baxter had said over the phone. Eight kilometres straight offshore to La Perousse Bank, a deep undersea shelf Baxter explained was rich with life due to upwelling currents. About an hour to go out and back. "Depends on the weather and if there's any fog and how much time you need." An hour hadn't sounded like much a month ago. He had made the call from the farmhouse after a day mending fences, warm after a shower, dressed in a T-shirt and comfortable jeans, beer in hand, supper on the way. A short boat ride. Today, eight kilometres felt like a hundred, and an hour an eternity. He struggled to control his breath. While on a rare vacation to the Qu'Appelle Valley with Uncle Pat and Aunt Gladys, Brent had built a raft out of old lumber, a tattered sheet for a sail. He had tried to convince Trevor to be first mate, but the adventure ended with Brent's taunt, "Baby Trevor scared of the water," while Trevor cried from a copse of poplars beyond the shore.

The unruffled voice of Constance interrupted the taunting. *What about the soul, Trevor, what about the soul?*

Was his life passing in front of him, the beginning of the end? Would he exit this life as fish food? He couldn't swim. You live and you die. He had said that, hadn't he? To Constance. What if there was more? A soul. An afterlife. Would he get another chance?

A favour for a friend.

When he opened his eyes, Trevor could no longer see land.

Ahead of them, a broad dense band of grey, twenty storeys high stretched across the horizon.

"What's that?" Trevor shouted to Baxter above the sound of the motors. "Ahead of us."

"Fog bank," Baxter yelled back.

"We can't go in there, can we?" Trevor said.

"No problem. GPS. You want to go to La Perousse, right?"

Trevor suspected his face matched the colour of the fog bank. He nodded, knuckles white from clutching the rope handhold that ran along the top of the pontoon.

They cruised straight into the wall of fog, as if motoring toward the edge of the world. Trevor feared the boat would carry on right over the lip, like a log over a waterfall. He shivered and hugged the vitamin bottle through the survival suit, wanting to tie himself to the rope fixed along the top of the pontoon, but the notion of what would happen if the boat should flip was enough to deter him.

Baxter slowed the inflatable and flicked switches. The boat didn't tip over the edge; instead, the world faded to monochrome. Shades of grey: green-grey water, dusky grey sky, metal-grey boat. Tattered wisps of fog drifted in the air between the two men. A heavy silence muffled the putter of the dampened motors. Trevor turned to discover that mist had obscured Baxter from view: his suit, the console of equipment had vanished. Trevor eased his foot along the floor to find the adjacent bench, which had also disappeared. He was alone. More alone than the night his parents had been killed, when he had Brent, relatives, neighbours. Today, his one companion was a stranger obscured in mist.

"Brent?'" His thin voice wobbled into the void.

"It's all right dear," Constance's voice reassured him. "Everyone has a grandmother."

Trevor strained toward the voice, trying to see through the grey wall. "Constance?"

"Not to worry, Mr. Wallace. It's only fog. But the name's Baxter, not Brent. We've got all the equipment, radar, GPS. I've done this a hundred times." The man's confidence descended over Trevor like angel song from heaven. "We're over the Bank. I'm shutting down the engines for a moment. If we're lucky, we might see whales. Porpoise. I heard there might be humpback around."

Trevor, disoriented, shook his head slowly back and forth. Baxter, yes Baxter. There were only two of them in the boat, Baxter and himself, Trevor Wallace. Did Baxter say they might see whales? He couldn't imagine how. The whiteout was reminiscent of a prairie snowstorm where you couldn't see your hand in front of your face. People died on their own doorsteps in stuff like this, lost in the blizzard inches from safety. The rescue people would find them in a few days, floating lifeless in their safety suits. Or not. Two men missing. Last seen heading out to La Perousse Bank from Ucluelet. Like the Bermuda Triangle. People and boats go in and never come out.

He slid cautiously across the bench toward the pontoon. An arm's reach away from the gunwhale, he leaned over, neck outstretched to peer over the edge. The fog undulated and opened like a curtain. The water shimmered like mercurial silver. He held his breath, loath to disturb the uncanny purity of the scene, then slid closer, reached over the side and swirled his fingers in the icy water.

He smelled the whale before he heard it, an overwhelming stench of salt and sea and watery flesh that made him gag and recoil to the centre of the boat. The cavern of fog filled with a mournful sigh.

"Humpback," Baxter whispered.

The water in front of the boat bubbled and fell away as a dense dark mass rose up and slid across the sea like a giant snake. Baxter and Trevor could see the pleated throat, the massive callused head—one eye searching, watching them—the stunted dorsal fin and the long fluted pectorals. The tail flukes curved up and over the heads of the men and sent a cascade of shining seadrops down in a glistening curtain. Then the giant vanished without a sound.

Trevor, thighs pressed against the flexible pontoon, gaped at the diminishing whirlpool, where in mere seconds, a leviathan had ascended and descended. Fog closed in over the spot. The boat rolled gently. Baxter materialized beside him and rested his warm hand on Trevor's shoulder.

"Now's a good time," he said.

The touch of the man's fingers was electric. Trevor turned and looked into Baxter's face. He wanted to hug him, tell him he'd never had a better friend. He wanted to talk about the wonder that just passed by them.

"A good time?"

When Baxter pointed at Trevor's hand, he remembered the ashes and the woman who had brought him here. It was time.

The mist shifted and a weak sunlight penetrated the fog in radiant fans. He pulled the plastic container from the bag. The word *Constance* was printed in neat, scarlet letters across the lid.

"She would have liked it here," he said out loud, but Baxter had returned to the fog.

Trevor unscrewed the lid and leaned over the side of the boat. "It was nice to know you, Constance. Thanks . . . for everything."

He overturned the dubious urn. Fine beige dust spilled out across the water surface and spread like weightless hieroglyphics on transparent papyrus. Trevor studied the lines and swirls. He could make no sense of the ephemeral shapes. It would be like Constance to leave him an undecipherable message in her passing. He dipped the container beneath the surface and it filled, the sea cold on his skin. With a swirl, he washed out the remaining ash.

A splash, a shout from Baxter and the bottle was torn from his fingers. A black and white fin, then another and another churned the water in front of him. Three animals dove and breached in circles around the floating ash. Six bright eyes observed Trevor as they darted by, air and water punching from their blowholes. The ash swirled down the tiny vortices created by the momentum of their sleek bodies, then they turned and sped away from the boat. Seawater sprayed over their backs in white sheets. Their dorsal fins flashed as they dove.

"Incredible," Baxter shouted. "Dall's porpoise. They like to bow ride, but I've never seen them do that."

Trevor hadn't moved. His skin tingled where the porpoise

had brushed his hand. The vitamin bottle was gone. Trevor searched the water near the boat. Did it sink? He ran his fingers through his hair. Or did they take it?

Baxter fired up the engines. "I have to get back for a tour."

They motored through the fog. When they broke through the grey wall into bright sunlight, Trevor squinted. Baxter donned his sunglasses. He gunned the engine and opened the throttle wide. The boat rose up to plane over the surface. Trevor felt almost airborne. He leaned back and soaked in the heat of the sun while he replayed the events of the last half-hour. The humpback. The three porpoises as they cavorted and dove. He pushed his next thought away, but the porpoises pushed it right back, their three curious pairs of eyes, checking him out, inviting him to join in. He shook his head. Impossible. Too far from comfortable territory. But Constance was famous for that, wasn't she? Pushing him into places he would never go on his own. Which one? Which one stole the bottle from his fingers? Martin? She would have liked that. Thomas, Donald and Martin come to collect her. Friendly guides to the afterlife.

He swivelled in his seat to watch the fog bank lift and thin in the morning sun. The rags of mist floated away and vanished until all that was left behind was the endless sweep of the ocean. Above, cerulean sky stretched forever west. Like the prairie sky. He raised his hand in farewell.

"See you, Constance," he whispered. "Somewhere, someday."

Ahead, the coast of Vancouver Island grew nearer, the tree-covered hills, the surf-washed shore, the scatter of buildings in the village of Ucluelet. Land. Where Angela waited at the hotel with a bottle of scotch.

ACKNOWLEDGEMENTS

I would like to thank the following people, all of whom surely have hearts as light as feathers, for the expertise and many hours they generously contributed to this book. Flowers for Ruth Linka at Brindle & Glass, who read an early draft and challenged me to rewrite and resubmit. Ruth shepherded the book through the publishing process with grace and good humour. Thanks also to my publicist, Emily Shorthouse, and editors Lynne Van Luven and Sarah Weber. My huge appreciations and admiration for the friends and colleagues who read drafts at many stages and provided invaluable comments, insights and prods: Pearl Arden, Tia Casper, Peggy Frank, Penny Joy, Leith Lesley, Gary and Barbara Moore, Lesley Pechter and Tory Stevens. You deserve medals. My parents Gay and Paul Eriksson read the book in its early stages and, as always, gave me gentle direction and encouragement.

My wonderful children, Noah and Camas, are never-ending fountains of inspiration and support. My beloved husband, Gary Geddes, who arrived in my life unexpectedly during the writing of this book, tiptoes into my studio with endless cups of tea and plates of food, and whispers in my ear, "keep on writing."

Should every writer be so lucky.

ANN ERIKSSON was born in Shaunavon, Saskatchewan and raised in all three Prairie provinces. She has worked as a biology consultant for the last fifteen years. Inspired by three close deaths in her family, she published her first novel *Decomposing Maggie* (2003), a moving and elegiac story about the management of grief. Ann is an environmentalist at heart and enjoys the outdoors and travel. She lives in Victoria, BC with her daughter Camas and her husband, poet Gary Geddes. Ann is currently working on two new novels. Please visit her website at www.anneriksson.ca.